Confetti

CONFETTI

A Collection of Cozy Crimes

Patricia L. Morin

Tayya Press
San Francisco, CA

As always, and forever, to my husband, Larry

Contents

Acknowledgments

With Gratitude:

Deke Castleman, my editor for over five years, and a constant source of insight on all levels of my work. Enjoy retirement.

Lourdes Venard, my new editor.

My critique group: Nicola Trwst, Judith Yamamoto, Shelley Singer, Bette Golden Lamb, and JJ Lamb. With a special thanks to Margaret Lucke for all that extra help.

Dr. Renee Brilliant, for our trip on the Cape May/ Lewes Ferry.

David from the Mizpah Volunteer Fire Department, Mizpah, NJ. Thank you for the information on your town.

Special thanks to the Sisters in Crime Northern California, the Hawaii Sisters in Crime, and the Sacramento Sisters in Crime for all their support!

My moral support team: Julie Benbow, Liz Hartka, Anthony Cohen, Beth Krieger, Adell Donaghue, Jennifer Berardi, Evan Berardi, and little Anya Berardi, along with my nieces, Cortney and Brianna Goodale.

Sue Trowbridge (interbridge.com), web designer and book formatter extraordinaire, and fellow theater lover.

Book cover design: Ronda Endress (ronda.endress@att.net)

Bookmarks and advertising: Ivy Woodruff

Introduction

In my first two books, *Mystery Montage* and *Crime Montage*, I responded to a fiction writer's most frequently asked question by readers: "Where do you get your ideas?" Many readers liked that I shared with them how my imagination grabbed different pieces of life, or experiences, or fantasies, and blended them into crime tales. So, once again in this third collection, I continue the practice.

"Pizza Man Murder" was written after an actual pizza deliverer, a young college kid, waited for us to pay for our pies. My husband, Larry, went to get the cash and I waited with the kid, and we started talking. After he heard what I did for a living, he said, "Hey, I could be a murderer!" I thought: "Hmm, now there's an idea."

"Bark Mitzvah Murder in Mizpah, NJ" is a humorous tale that I wrote for Deadly Ink Publisher's yearly short-story collection. The short story had to take place in New Jersey, where I was born and lived for my first eighteen years. I first thought of a bark mitzvah after I spotted doggie costumes in a pet shop. A man in the pet shop talked about his dog that was thirteen. My friend's daughter was becoming bat mitzvahed in a few days. Bingo. Then I Googled towns in New Jersey with the letter M, and found, to my amazement, Mizpah, a town two miles long not far from Atlantic City. It was meant to be!

"A Hui Hou Kakou" takes place on the island of Oahu, where I lived for five years. My fear of drowning in those large waves came alive when I wrote about Lexi (a young surfer) and her drowning incident in the huge winter waves at Sunset Beach. I was asked to write a short story for a Hawaii anthology, *Sunset Inn: Tales from the North Shore*, and the story was already written!

"Murder Interrupted Me" was born from an idea I had about fishing, and how many anglers love the relaxation of fishing more than actually catching fish. This story was accepted in the Sacramento Sisters in Crime anthology *Capitol Crimes*.

"Love Shack" was inspired by an experiment I wanted to try. I wanted half of a story to be a dream, and the other half of the story to be the reality that actualizes from that dream. Neither worked out, but the theme remained. This short story was chosen for another Hawaii anthology, *Mystery in Paradise: 13 Tales of Suspense*.

"LA Car" takes place near Venice Beach, CA, and the story wraps around a car-themed restaurant where remote-control cars deliver your drinks on the beach. My husband and I were on that beach and I thought, wouldn't it be cool if they had remote-control delivery vehicles? I first thought of remote control planes, but, well, you can only imagine.

"Psychic Spies" was entered into the MWA *Cold War* anthology. I loved researching the history of "Star Wars" and all the paranormal activity that was studied and utilized during 1979 (the year I chose to write about). The story was featured in the summer edition of the Mill Valley Literary Review webzine.

"Harry and Penny" is a PI humorous mystery and explores the relationship between a brother and sister who have worked together for many years—and how people create their own form of communication. This story was chosen for *The House With Many Rooms* anthology by Weaving Dreams Publishing, but has yet to be released.

"The Ferry" is a novella about love and grief, ambivalence, and the resolution of a lost relationship. The underlining theme is freedom. It began as a short literary story that kept nagging at me to write more. I actually rode on the Cape May-Lewes car ferry, and ambled through their gift shop. However, I don't have a sister, and the gift shop attendant, when I was riding the ferry, was nothing like "Joe."

Thank you for reading my work. I hope you enjoy the stories. If you would like to learn more about me, and my work, please check out my website: www.patricialmorin.com.

Pizza Man
Murder

The news bounced off the TV satellite down through cold, gray, snow clouds that spewed early-winter flakes, into Kyle Canyon, and past the huge evergreens that lined the hillside like soldiers at attention. The large-screen TV blared the news so that all four family members in the large log cabin could hear it from four different rooms. "Another body has been found which police are initially treating as the seventh victim of the so-called Pizza Man serial killer. A traffic helicopter spotted the car on a remote side road in Lee Canyon, eight miles south of US95. Though the body remains unidentified, sources close to the investigation have confirmed that the automobile in which it was found in the backseat belongs to fifty-two-year-old Hector Schmitt of North Las Vegas ..."

Short redheaded Edna, with her fiery gray eyes and buck teeth, grabbed the remote and muted the television. "One week!" she yelled at her husband, Don, even though he was sitting right next to her on the living room sofa. "That man's body was in the car for a full week before they found him!"

"Probably frozen in this cold snap," Don leaned back and breathed easy. "Whoever heard of snow and temperatures in the twenties this close to Las Vegas? Turn on the heat, for God's sake, Edna. Or we'll all be just as stiff as that corpse."

The doorbell rang. Edna jumped up off the couch.

"Pizza delivery!" a deep voice yelled out.

Edna turned to her husband, eyes wide. "Did you order a pizza, Don?"

He reached for the remote to turn the sound back on. "No, dear. I didn't order a pizza, but boy, I could go for a nice large pepperoni right about now," he said sarcastically. "Maybe we should just let him in and see what he brought." Don chuckled as he flicked his dark hair out of his even darker eyes.

"Wait! I'll go check with the kids and see if they ordered a pizza without telling us. We have to be careful with all that's happening."

Edna had run halfway up the stairs before she heard more pounding on the front door.

"Pizza delivery!" the deep voice yelled out again, even louder and, now, annoyed.

"Hurry up, ask the kids," Don said in a stage whisper, then approached the door. "Be right there! Hold your horses!" he shouted, as if the pizza man was hard of hearing.

Edna leaped the final steps two at a time. She hurried into the room her fifteen-year-old son occupied. Junior sat in front of the computer, engrossed in a Captain America movie, red wavy hair uncombed, a Navy jacket on, and Thinsulate gloves covering both hands.

"Did you order a pizza, Junior?" she demanded.

"No, Mom," he responded with his back to her. "But I sure would like a couple slices of chicken barbecue, if someone else did."

"Yeah, I know you would," Edna turned to leave.

"It's freezing in here, Mom. Turn on the heat!"

She scooted into the next room, where thirteen-year-old Sis stretched her lean body on the bed, long dark hair ruffled on the pillow, school books scattered around her, texting on her iPad.

"Sis!" Edna caught her attention. "There's a pizza man at the door."

"No, Mom, I didn't order a pizza!" Sis glared at her mother. "But would you please turn up the heat? If you don't, I will! I'm sure Junior and Dad are freezing, too."

Edna scanned the room. "How can you get anything done in this pigsty! If I told you once, I told you a thousand times!"

"You are so compulsive. It's a disease, Mom. You know it?" Then she softened and grinned, then said, "I really could go for a vegetarian. I'm hungry. Go check, Mom."

Edna raced down the steps, shaking her head at Don, who was watching her closely.

"Well, Let's just see what he brought us. "

Edna stared at Don. "Do you think it's safe? This Pizza Man killer is on the news again! And the last body was found not too far from here."

"Well, the door's chained. While I go get the gun, why don't you open it a crack and ask him for his ID to make sure it's not the wrong pizza man?"

Don left the room as Edna stood by the door. "Are you sure this is the right address?" she yelled through the door.

"Yes!" The delivery guy repeated the address. "It's freezing out here, lady! You ordered four large pies, or someone in this house did! Now, you either open this door right now or I'm leaving! I mean it! I want to get home before the storm hits!"

Edna opened the door and peered out. "What's your name?"

"My name? What's that got to do with your bill of sixty-two dollars and twenty-three cents?"

"Just making sure."

"It's George. George Wynn."

Don stood behind her, .45 semi-automatic in hand, as Edna opened the door.

"Finally!" A middle-aged man with thick wet glasses, a snow-covered mustache, and a stack of pizza boxes stepped inside.

"Yep," Edna answered. "I ordered the pizza. And yep, you're the right pizza man." She stretched her arms toward him to take the four boxes.

As George Wynn was handing them to her, Don raised the gun and hit him over the head, hard.

The man's look of horror went blank as he fell to the floor.

"Junior! Get down here and help me with the body."

"About time, Dad. Jesus. I'm starved." Junior trotted down the steps.

"This time, let's put George Wynn in the trunk of his delivery car."

"Sis," Edna said to the girl coming down the stairs, "bring these to the kitchen."

"Great. Let's eat. I'm starving, and we can warm our hands on the pizza." She grabbed the boxes.

"All right." Edna followed Sis into the kitchen. "But let's hurry up. We don't have much time. And don't touch anything! I have enough fingerprints to wipe off as it is."

"You did order the vegetarian with extra cheese, didn't you, Mom?"

"Of course I did. Do I ever do anything differently on these jobs? You know how compulsive I am, and it's not going to stop. It hasn't failed us yet, has it? Did you clean your room? Pack your pillow and the extra sheet on the bed? I don't want you leaving any of your DNA around."

"Uh huh." Sis chewed her piece, swallowed, then added, "Mom, I did everything we always do when we break into someone's house. I hate this one. Next time, a bigger one, in a warm place."

"Talk to Junior. He does the casing."

"I liked it better when Dad did it." Sis pulled the two-liter Pepsi bottle from the brown paper bag.

Don and Junior stomped their plastic-covered boots on the porch floor before they came into the house. "Let's make it a quick dinner, then hit the road," Don said, sitting down and opening the box with his pepperoni. "We need to outrun this storm."

Junior grabbed a slice of chicken barbecue. "Who was this guy, Dad?"

"This guy? George Wynn? His real name is, or was, George Drysdale. He was serving a life sentence in Arizona for the murder of a twelve-year-old girl, Jenna Syreen, who was walking the family poodle in front of her home."

Sis stopped eating and looked at her father. "Where in Arizona?"

Don paused, then said, "Mesa."

"Mesa! That's only a few miles from where Sarah was kidnapped! Do you think he might be...?"

"We'll never know if he's the one, Sis. But we do know that he'll never do a little girl any harm ever again."

"How much is he worth?" Junior wanted to know.

Don glanced at Edna. "Twenty-five thousand," she said.

"Twenty-five thousand!" Junior exclaimed.

"We're going after the bigger rewards now," Edna said. "We have to think about your college tuition."

"So? Who's next?" Sis asked.

"Well," Don said, "we're running out of pizza men. Since we started this project last year, pizza places are checking the background of their delivery drivers more closely. Now it's time to move up."

"Move up?" Junior said.

"Yes," Edna said. "The jobs will get more dangerous, but they're worth a lot more money."

"Who are they?" Sis asked.

Don finished chewing, put down his slice of his pepperoni, and said, "Other bounty hunters."

Bark Mitzvah Murder in Mizpah, New Jersey

"Come on, Irv, walk faster. We're already late." Rena nudged her sixty-eight-year-old-husband to quicken his pace.

"Who knew Mizpah was only two square miles? Not like our Ventnor City. I drove right past it!"

"Just hurry!"

"I can't believe you're dragging me to this preposterous party, Rena," Irv complained, hot and bothered from walking to the house. "Who ever heard of a so-called rabbi blessing a thirteen-year-old mutt! Ach, what's this world coming to?"

"You know this crowd and their theme parties, honey," Rena smiled at her husband of forty years, her typical way of dispelling his bad moods. "And you have to admit, this bark mitzvah is a great way for friends to get together and have some fun."

"Some fun," Irv grumbled. "I'm still not over the Fourth of July beach party in Joe and Edna's backyard. When old Edna came out wearing that red, white, and blue bikini, God in heaven! After that, I couldn't eat. Not a thing, I tell you."

"Aren't some of the houses on this street beautiful, honey? So nice of Ricky's friends to let them have the bark mitzvah in their new home."

"Hard to see through all these trees, Rena."

The huge custom-built pale-blue and white Victorian, with one corner spire and circular driveway, took Rena's breath away. The mansion was decorated with handcrafted filigree and the windows and the doors were trimmed out with layers of molding, all painted in varying shades of blue. "Oh, Irving, look at those stained-glass windows on the second and third floors. Aren't they beautiful?"

"Yes, dear. Let's go in. I'm thirsty." He started up the seven white steps to the wicker-filled wraparound porch, carrying the big camera bag over his shoulder.

Rena itched to pull out her camera and start shooting. She loved the outrageous parties her nephew, Ricky, and his partner, Shogo, threw. What imaginations! She could just picture all the vivid decorations to go with the color scheme inspired by their brown poodle, Sam. And Ricky's friends were such characters! Rena ran her hands along her long brown-and-white-striped dress, and fixed her brown fifties hat with a matching brown veil on her highlighted short brown-and-auburn wavy hair. Reaching for the white handrail with carved spindles, she watched Irv climb the steps. Their daily three-mile walks kept them in shape, the older-model shape.

Irv waited for her at the top of the stairs. "Sam Spade. Such a horrible name for a mutt."

"Wait till you show your friends all the pictures on your iPhone at the Beach Deli tomorrow morning. You'll be the hit of breakfast."

"Maybe. But I'm not dancing. I'm telling you now, not one step. No way. So don't ask."

"Oh, stop your moaning. You always have a good time, and you always dance. I hate when you act like an old man!"

The noise level signaled that the party had begun. Above the hubbub, Nat King Cole's song "Unforgettable" played from a real piano.

Walking in, Rena spotted Ricky right away, standing in the middle of the large living room. As if on a psychic swivel, Ricky's head snapped around and he shouted, "Aunt Rena! Uncle Irv! Thank you so much for coming!"

He was tall, thin, and clean-shaven, with green-gray eyes and wavy chestnut hair. Dressed in a brown tux with a white ruffle shirt, he was so handsome! Rena would snap his picture first.

Greeting them at the door, Ricky hugged them both, then lifted the camera bag from Irv's shoulder. "Take a load off, Uncle Irv. Let's go set up Aunt Rena by the bar. It's over there." He pointed to the right, behind a long half-wall to the dining room, temporarily converted into a bar area, with two brown linen tablecloth-covered serving stations against the back wall and a dance floor in front of the windows.

Rena scanned the dining room, with its floor-to-ceiling windows that looked out to an inground swimming pool, a small vegetable garden to the right, and a peek-a-boo view of the flower garden on the back left. She could snap some nice frames indoors, and the guests silhouetted against the big windows would be lovely.

Her camera accompanied her, like a friend, to all the crime scenes she photographed for the Hamilton County Police Department, including some Atlantic City casinos. But unlike her friends, her camera never lied. If my camera could talk, she thought, the dead would rise and crowd the earth, especially after thirty years of photographing homicides, suicides, and all the bodies that had fallen by unnatural and natural means behind the yellow caution tape.

"Oh, Rena, honey, don't you look wonderful!" Short, well-built, and Asian-American, Shogo approached them with a wide smile. "Love the retro hat, and those shoes!"

"Consignment shop, Second Time Around the Block. I'll take you there next time you come over." Rena fingered the 100-percent polyester fabric of his Nehru suit. "Haven't seen one of these since the seventies. Love the paisley. Where's Sam?"

"Oh, he's playing on the side of the house. We only invited his five closest doggie friends."

"Good thinking."

Ricky set the camera bag down on a table next to the bar. "First, drinks all around," he said. "Then I'll show Irv to the home-theater room."

"Perfect plan." Irv brightened a bit. "Bar first. Sports second."

While the boys were busy at the bar, Rena's photographer's eye took in the long table in front of the half-wall, piled with gifts wrapped in brown-and-white stripes, dots, grocery bags, and white with brown bows. In front of the table were thirteen chairs, for part of Sammy's actual little ceremony. To the left of the piano, where an Elvis impersonator played background music, stood a tall African-American man talking to a beautiful woman dressed in a long silk dark-chocolate gown with a figure that filled it out perfectly.

"Thank you for the marvelous pictures of Sam winning the blue ribbon!" Shogo said, handing her a glass of white wine. "Sam's breeding prices have skyrocketed now that he's placed first three times. I'm so excited! And isn't this setting simply exquisite?"

"It certainly is, darling. Whose home is it?"

"Donna and David. David's probably upstairs, giving a tour. But that's Donna over there, talking to the rabbi."

Rena, expecting an older man in a suit and yarmulke, looked to see where Shogo was pointing. "The black guy?"

"Okay, Auntie, get that camera out and I'll go through the list of important guests. We need photos of everyone!" Shogo said pointing his thin, manicured finger toward the piano.

In one swift move, Rena withdrew her camera, had the viewfinder to her eye, and clicked an unexpected quick candid shot of Shogo, before he could morph into a more dramatic pose for a second shot.

He laughed, then said, "Jeremiah begged us to be the rabbi. He loves to be the center of attention."

Click-click. "Looks like a young Will Smith."

"Everyone says that. She's one of the country's top dog handlers. The judges can't take their eyes off her. She would win most of her shows. Except for Judge Danny."

Click-click-click. "Stunning long black hair, and she has blue eyes."

"Now, at the piano is ... well, never mind his real name.

He lives in the house next to ours. Just moved in. He's an impersonator. Obviously. Gay, too."

Click-click. "Looks great! Could pass as Elvis's twin."

"Over there, standing by the buffet table are two other important doggie-show people. Stuffy SOBs, but we had to invite them just the same. The one on the left, delicious! Co-co crisp, with those luscious lips and caramel eyes, and that button nose, and cute ... well, never mind. That's Griffin Knapp. He's a bitch, but I wouldn't mind taking a nap with him."

Click-click. Shogo liked to flirt, Rena knew, but Ricky never seemed to mind. "I think the rabbi's cuter."

"Griffin's straight, though. Rumor has it he has the hots for Donna. Now, the one on the right is Judge Danny. He can't stand Donna, and she feels the same way about him. Everyone knows he won't pick her dog if she's in the competition. Nasty. He's also mad that his fat Chow, who looks like him with all that brown kinky hair and black eyes, wasn't invited. But Sam doesn't really like the Chow. He's too much of a sniffer, catching every dog's telephone number, if you know what I mean, like all day long!"

Click-click. "Oh, stop! He's not that bad. His hair is a bit ... unruly." Click.

"Does anyone know that Sam's only seven and not thirteen?"

"It'll be our little secret, honey," Shogo whispered. "Sam's so sensitive about his age."

Suddenly, Shogo gasped and his eyes went wide. "Oh my God! Where are the flowers for the piano?"

Rena pointed her camera at the piano. She snapped Jeremiah, the rabbi, having words with Elvis. Jeremiah looked angry and was shaking his index finger in Elvis's face.

"I'll be back. I have to track down the florist. They were supposed to be here over an hour ago! Make yourself at home, honey. You simply must check out the buffet. The salmon's to die for and the grilled asparagus with goat cheese, yummy. I'll catch you later." Shogo scooted toward the front door, stopped, and loudly announced. "The ceremony will begin in a half-hour! Please get your guest puppies ready!"

Rena started picking her way through the crowd, heading toward the buffet table, snapping a few frames as she went. A hand touched her shoulder and she looked around at Ricky, returning to her side. "Are most of the people here your friends?" she asked. "I don't recognize anyone."

"You're right. Most of them are just acquaintances from the dog shows. Who else would come to a bark mitzvah?"

Rena laughed, thinking about Irv, drinking his beer and watching a game.

"The Elvis impersonator is our neighbor. Jeremiah over there," he pointed, "is a friend of Shogo's from the club. Shogo introduced Jeremiah to Danny over there," he pointed again, "who's the dog-show judge. Oh, and the caterer is a friend of ours. You'll recognize her from some of the other parties."

"Tall blonde with funky glasses and the apron with strawberries all over it? Great pies? Jeanie?"

"I see your memory for visuals is sharper than ever, Aunt Rena." Ricky beamed.

"You know, I just snapped a picture of Elvis and the, uh, rabbi, and they didn't look too happy with each other."

"Oh yeah, we have several drama queens, besides Shogo, who always makes me smile when he's on show.

But these guys, I don't know. At the last dog party, the tension was so high, we swore one of them was going to be murdered. Worse than *Downton Abbey*."

"Really?" Rena's police-department antennae started to quiver. "Like who?"

"Well, Danny and Jeremiah are the couple from hell. Danny's, uh, difficult, and it's no secret that he's making a play for, uh, Elvis. So Elvis and Jeremiah were probably bickering over that."

Rena glanced over at Judge Danny, then at Jeremiah the rabbi.

"Yeah, I know what you're thinking." Ricky shrugged. "Makes the world go round."

"Well, I think I'll roam about and take some more pictures. How's Irv?"

"No worries. His TV buddy from the blue-ribbon party is here. They're drinking beers and talking sports. You have your script for the candle-lighting ceremony?"

"I do. But where are the other twelve guests?"

"Oh, we hired a friend of Elvis's, a female impersonator, to play the parts of ten of them. Very funny. So, in order, it's Judge Danny, you, Elvis, and the impersonator."

"How clever of you both, dear! Well, I'm off to snap pictures. It's so great to photograph live people. I just love candids."

"Remember to take pictures of all the dogs, Auntie. Shogo will have a snit-fit if you don't, and I'll hear about it for weeks."

***

For twenty minutes Rena snapped pictures, a voyeur into other's people lives for a change, a nice break from their deaths, focusing on expressions, gestures, body language, and frozen moments in time. Click-click-click.

She snacked on two sundried-tomato-and-cream-cheese rosemary crackers, a deviled egg with paprika, and snuck two grilled eggplants, onions, and peppers tapas. Then she studied her shots in the frame of the camera. Two women who looked like sisters whispering about something scandalous. They sat at one of the round banquet tables, knees touching. She zoomed in on the touching knees.

Elvis crooning "Song Sung Blue," almost making love to the microphone.

Jeremiah, the unlikely rabbi, reading his script at the dais.

Donna, posing like a model holding her drink, smiling at her.

Judge Danny popping a peppermint Tic Tac, while talking to the stunningly handsome Griffin Knapp.

Photographs, some of them hers, hanging on the wall behind the long table stacked with gifts.

The gifts.

The empty thirteen light-oak chairs.

An underdressed woman in blue jeans and a brown sweatshirt.

Judge Danny pointing to the salmon paté.

The dessert table with two cakes: one vanilla with a poodle etched in brown frosting and Happy Birthday on it, the other a chocolate mousse with thirteen candles.

Griffin Knapp, now sitting with a young twenty-something man and woman at one of the tables, staring at Donna.

David upstairs in his study, writing in a notebook.

David waving.

Jeanie the caterer, in her strawberry apron, coming out of a bathroom upstairs near the study.

Ricky raising his glass to Irv and his TV pal as he walked into the Great Room.

A woman with blonde stringy hair and round glasses staring longingly at the pool.

Jeremiah the rabbi and Judge Danny smiling at each other, with Elvis staring in the background.

David and Jeanie walking down the steps smiling, hands almost touching.

Griffin Knapp kissing Donna's hand.

The front of the house.

The florist, carrying two big bouquets through the front door.

Irv bringing her a drink.

Ricky and Irv, side by side.

Donna and Judge Danny having a major disagreement.

Ricky and Shogo, with Donna frowning at Judge Danny in the background.

Elvis, Judge Danny, and Griffin Knapp holding plates and conversing in the buffet line.

Shogo clapping his hands for everyone's attention.

Jeanie and Ricky talking.

Shogo shouting, and clapping his hands for everyone's attention.

The sisters still whispering, knee to knee, a tissue in one of their hands.

David's arm around a smiling Donna.

Jeanie and Jeremiah whispering.

A stern-looking Irv clapping his hands for everyone's attention.

The ceremony is beginning, Rena thought. She'd take pictures of the ceremony and people's reactions.

Men donned brown-and-white-spotted yarmulkes.

Shogo and Ricky left the room, as the other breeders and show people entered, holding Sam's small playmates. Rena stood in the back near the buffet table, snapping pictures of all the dogs and their masters, as Ricky had requested.

Irv came to stand by her side.

Elvis played light piano music as Ricky and Shogo carried Sam in a custom-made doggie-crafted chaise upholstered with crushed brown velvet. Sam was panting, and his deep brown eyes wandered around the guests as if he was accustomed to being honored. With Ricky on his right and Shogo on his left, they approached Jeremiah.

Elvis stopped playing, and Jeremiah the rabbi cleared his throat. "On behalf of Sam Spade and his parents, Ricky and Shogo, we thank you, beloved friends, for honoring us with your presence on this special occasion, Sam's thirteenth birthday and bark mitzvah. I will now bestow a blessing on you all." Then he spoke some foreign-sounding words.

Irv whispered to Rena, "that's not Hebrew. What language is that?"

"Gibberish, Irv. He's not a real rabbi."

"My mother's turning in her grave," Irv said. "Yours, too."

"With all the antics that go on in your family, I'm surprised she didn't install a turnstile in her coffin."

"Don't be such a smart aleck." Irv sighed. "How long is this ceremony, anyway?"

"Well, Judge Danny is going to talk about his first show win. And I have to give a speech about Sam's first training class. Then Elvis sings him a song."

"Oy vey." Irv shook his head. "I'm getting us another drink."

"I don't want another drink."

"I'll drink it for you then." Irv snuck behind the crowd and toward the bar.

"Now we all will join around the cake table, where our thirteen guests will speak about Sam and light the candles."

The crowd followed Ricky and Shogo, still carrying the chaise.

A heavyset woman wearing a brown polka-dot dress and a fake white wig, smelling of lilacs, blocked Rena's view. "Are you the female impersonator?" Rena asked.

"Yes," a male voice responded. "I'm late. I missed the town and wound up in Mays Landing."

"Well, at least you made it in time. The Judge gives a little talk, then I give a little talk, then Elvis sings, then you're on."

"Is the judge the tall fat guy, with the windblown hair?"

"Yes, the one next to the, uh, rabbi, getting ready to speak."

"Oh good, I have a few minutes then. I need something to eat, and a drink."

"The food is delicious. You must try the asparagus and goat cheese. To die for."

The impersonator slipped by her, making a beeline for the buffet table.

Jeremiah spoke to the crowd. "Our first speaker is the renowned dog-show judge of judges: Judge Danny."

Applause.

Click-click.

"Ladies and gentleman!" Judge Danny spoke in a commanding voice. "I've known Sam Spade for four years now and he's always been a winner. He walks with pride, his head and tail up high. His patience is limitless, his temperament even, and look at the shine on that coat!" His arm swept out, like an award-show host introducing a movie queen. But suddenly, his smile turned into a grimace and his arm sprung back, grabbing for his chest. He turned red and wheezed, his mouth twisted in a scowl, then Judge Danny wavered, tipped over, and fell face forward, his chest flattening the birthday cake on the dessert table.

The crowd froze, then started to hum. Rena's training kicked in and she clicked the entire scene.

Jeremiah calling 911.

Irv yelling, "Move back! And someone help me place him on the floor!"

Ricky handing the chaise to Shogo.

Shogo placing it on the chair, Sam jumping off of it to investigate.

Ricky, Irv, and Shogo gingerly lifting Judge Danny, exposing his chest plastered with cake, and lowering him to the floor.

Sam licking the vanilla icing off of Judge Danny's chest.

Shogo shooing him away.

Judge Danny, on his back, a bloodless pallor to his face.

Then she lowered the camera. Poor Judge Danny, Rena thought as she watched the commotion with two eyes instead of one. And the boys, too. Their wonderful bark mitzvah ruined by ... what? A random misfortune? A twist of fate? A premeditated act?

Irv listened for a heartbeat and felt for a pulse. "Doesn't look good."

"Danny, Danny!" Jeremiah knelt by his side. "Get him a blanket and a pillow! Oh my poor Danny!"

"I'll get them!" David ran up the steps.

"I'll help," Donna followed.

"I'll get towels to clean him up," Jeanie said from behind the dessert table.

"Do you need me to help lift his head?" Elvis knelt down on the other side.

"No, too many people," Irv waved Elvis away, then undid Judge Danny's shirt buttons.

David and Donna brought a blanket and pillow as Irv lifted Judge Danny's head and David covered his body. Some of the guests stood by the bar. Others shuffled toward the door, saying goodbye to Ricky and Shogo, now standing on the porch.

Rena heard sirens in the distance, growing louder by the second. She knew the Hamilton County PD would be notified, routine in these emergency cases. She moved to a corner of the bar area, sat down, and scanned all the photographs on the camera. Her eyes narrowed as her thumb pushed the picture-forward button. Her nose crinkled as she reviewed all the frames two more times.

The ambulance and police arrived simultaneously. She went out to greet them.

The medics jumped into action, and Irv updated them, describing the apparent heart attack. Jeremiah confirmed that Judge Danny had a heart problem. The medics loaded him onto a gurney and wheeled him to the ambulance.

Rena pulled aside the woman police officer, Officer Meacham, and showed her all the photographs, explained her suspicions, and asked her to call Rena's boss at the station to verify her identity.

"That won't be necessary. I know who you are. Everyone in the department knows you," Meacham said as she studied the frames intently. "So what do you want me to do?"

Rena explained.

Meacham nodded. "Don't see any harm in that. Clever, actually. I'll call for backup from Homicide, then go in and talk to them."

Officer Meacham called everyone together as the ambulance pulled away.

"I want to follow the ambulance," Jeremiah said. "He's my partner."

"I want to follow the ambulance," Elvis said. "He's going to be my partner."

"All of you, sit down." Officer Meacham pointed to the thirteen chairs. Rena and Irv, Ricky and Shogo, Elvis and Jeremiah, David and Donna, Jeanie, and Griffin Knapp sat on the chairs. The last guests, the impersonator, and Irv's TV buddy waved back at them as they left, cake plates in hand. Sam jumped up on the empty chair next to Rena. She stroked him, and waited.

"We have a problem here, folks," Officer Meacham said, the husky voice a bit strange coming from someone so petite and graceful. Her long brown hair was tied in a ponytail down her back, and her aviator sunglasses hid her eyes. "Judge Danny, as you call him, had a minute of consciousness in the ambulance. His eyes fluttered, he coughed, and he whispered something to the medic, words that implicate one of you in something very suspicious."

Everyone glanced at one another.

Rena knew that no cop would say that, but none of these people would suspect it, and Meacham acted her role very well.

"Now, you two," she pointed to Irv and Rena, "just met him today and didn't know he even had a heart problem."

Rena and Irv nodded.

"Everyone else did."

They all nodded.

"Does anybody want to confess to giving the judge anything that might have brought on his heart attack?"

Everyone shook their heads.

"Does anyone want to confess to switching a pill or spiking his drink?"

Everybody shook their heads.

She's doing a great job, Rena thought. The next question should really zero in on the killer.

"Did you all know he carried Tic Tacs in his pocket?"

David, Jeanie, Shogo, and Ricky shook their heads. At the same time, Donna, Griffin, Elvis, and Jeremiah nodded impulsively, before realizing they might be implicating themselves in foul play. Rena observed closely, watching to see who looked most nervous.

David and Donna glanced at each other.

Jeremiah glared at Elvis.

"So what if we did?" Griffin demanded. "No crime in that."

"I love him," Elvis insisted. "He's going to be my boyfriend."

"I love him, too," Jeremiah added. "He is my boyfriend."

Meacham let the room simmer down, then said, "One last general question for all of you." She paused.

Let them wait for it, Rena thought. She could hear a car door slam.

The detective. Perfect timing. Meacham had held out just long enough and the homicide detective came quickly.

She had fed him his one and only sentence when she called in for backup.

"Last question here, Detective." Meacham stated as the detective moseyed in.

He nodded.

"Which one of you has the most to lose if he stays alive?"

"Donna does!" Jeremiah yelled. "Everyone knows her dogs never win when Danny's a judge!"

"I did not kill him!"

"My wife did not kill Judge Danny!" David stood and pointed his finger in the officer's face.

"Sit down before I arrest you!" Meacham yelled back.

"For what?"

"Obstructing a murder investigation," the detective, stepping between them, said quietly.

"Murder!" Griffin Knapp gasped.

"Yes. The police have just been informed that Daniel Stuart passed on the way to the hospital." He removed handcuffs from his belt. "I'm sorry, ma'am, but you'll have to come with me."

"No, no! Please! I didn't do it." Donna started to cry.

Everyone stood now. Shogo and Ricky edged closer to David and Donna.

"No, don't take her!" Griffin yelled above the clamor. "I did it! I did it for her!"

The detective turned to Griffin. "What did you do?

"I didn't mean to kill him! I didn't want him to die! I thought I gave him the right amount ... just a little speed coated with peppermint ... I looked up how much on Google!" Griffin stood and curled his fist in anguish.

"Why'd you do it?" the detective asked, moving toward him with the cuffs.

"She was going to lose her job. I'd never see her again. Never! I just wanted him to be out of the show ring for a while. I love you, Donna!" He reached out to her.

She turned and threw herself into David's arms.

"You have the right to remain silent. Anything you say ..."

"I wasn't going to murder him! You have to believe me!" Griffin yelled as the detective cuffed him.

Officer Meacham and Rena smiled at each other.

"Thank you for those suggestions. You were spot on, and I'll be damned if it didn't work!" Meacham gave her a high-five.

"Rena, this is the quickest case I ever worked on. Thanks." The detective handed Griffin off to Meacham.

"Did Judge Danny really die?" Rena asked.

The detective shook his head. "But they say it's touch and go." He walked out, gripping Griffin Knapp by the arm.

"We're going to the hospital," Elvis said, leaving with Jeremiah.

"How did you ever figure this out?" Ricky asked.

"I'll show you the pictures later. It was really a guess. See, I took shots of Griffin, while Donna and Judge Danny were arguing. I was shocked by the look of hatred in his eyes. I began to suspect he switched the Tic Tacs when he stood behind Judge Danny at the buffet table. I wasn't certain, but my hunch turned out to be right."

"Thank you so much," Donna hugged her. "I thought the police were going to arrest me."

"That was staged. Sorry about that, dear."

"Poor Judge Danny," David said woefully. "Right in the middle of his bark mitzvah speech. I hope he makes it."

Rena nodded, glanced at Irv, who smiled at her with pride and love.

Ricky, over at the stereo, said, "Let's put some music on while we clean up."

"Put on some ABBA," Shogo called over. "That's Sam's favorite. It's still his bark mitzvah, after all." Shogo snapped his fingers and danced a few steps swinging his hips.

Sam barked, and Shogo picked him up and danced with him in his arms.

Rena put her arm through Irv's, and locked onto his eyes.

"Okay, you twisted my arm. Just one dance, you hear me? Just one. No more than that."

"We'll see."

A Hui Hou Kakou (Till We Meet Again)

I drowned. It wasn't as bad as I thought drowning would be, really.

It's the gurgling, and the salt water rushing into your nose and mouth, that's hard at first. It burns. You think if you gasp you'll get air, but it doesn't come. I breathed in salt water and it burned my nose, throat, lungs, and stomach.

What happened? I don't remember exactly. I was angling my surfboard into a wave near the pipeline on Sunset Beach when suddenly I was exhausted. The wave broke on me and down I went. The undertow pulled me deep. I didn't hold my breath immediately, something I always did on instinct, but coughed underwater. Salt water poured into me.

I panicked. I tried to yell for help. The muffled sounds surrounded my head, and then there was silence.

A bright light shone down on me through the aquamarine water.

The surface never seemed far away.

Worried voices shouted my name.

Then I was calm. My body stopped moving, but my ears heard everything. Fish nibbled at the coral. It was a soft crackling sound, almost like they were whispering to one another. The fish were so beautiful; parrots, groupers, and angelfish were all staring at me.

But as my body smacked against the coral, they swam away. I was dying. I no longer had control of anything but my mind.

Dying is peaceful when you're floating.

I thought about Mom at her florist shop in town, probably talking to her boyfriend Zach, who owned the flower farm and the warehouse where she bought her flowers. Then Dad popped into my head. Did he know I was dead? Did Mom?

There was Keoki and our marriage when I turned twenty-one in May, Ko Maua la Male 'ana, our wedding day. It was to be my birthday present the day after our college graduation. We were to elope.

I loved Keoki so much. If I could feel my heart, it would have been sick.

If I could touch my eyes, tears would have been flowing into the salty sea.

The image of his face, his smile, and his loving brown eyes subdued me like the warm powerful currents washing over me.

A hui hou kakou. Until we meet again.

I thought I heard chimes. That was before the darkness. That was before Tutu Styles greeted me at the end of the tunnel and sent me back. Her long gray hair draped her shoulders, her lips pursed in frown, and her thin, boney finger pointed into the darkness. "Lexi, go back, help your mother," she said. "She needs you."

***

I woke up coughing. My eyes burned and I could feel air in my lungs. My body hurt. There were hushed voices around me, one low and deep, and one soft and high.

Fish whispers.

Mom was crying hard. I knew the sound of her tears. I could smell her Hawaiian gardenia-scented perfume. Then I felt her hug me so tight that the deep voice told her to move away. I was in a ... a ... hos ... pi ... tal. I know it's a place for sick people. Right? They were whispering above me, sounds floating in and out, high and low. They were the fish at the coral, whispering.

Mom just cried.

"Oh honey. I was so worried about you. I love you honey, my sweetest flower. I thought you were gone forever, forever from me." Mom kissed me all over my face. It was hard to breathe. My eyelashes flickered adjusting to the light; my eyes hurt.

"Mrs. Evans. Please move away." The doctor pulled her back.

I squeezed her hand and smiled a little.

***

We came home the next day. Mom closed her shop and stayed by my side. I sensed something heavy in the air, something mom wanted to share, but didn't. Then she said my medical tests came back and that my thinking would be messed up for a while. My brain got waterlogged. I didn't feel it swishing in my head, but I got tired when I did too much thinking. I seemed younger, like I was in eighth grade again or something. Everything was foggy and strange, like I was still floating in the misty water. Some of mom's words flowed in the air around me, like drifting in a lazy stream.

***

Keoki came over and he looked worried. I hugged him. He smiled down at me and I grabbed his hand. We walked outside and stood under the palm tree next to the Sunset Inn. A rainbow had formed from the rainy mist across the water. I knew that meant good luck. Keoki leaned into me. His brown eyes studied me like he was reading a book. Then they studied my eyes, probing into my brain.

"Hey, Blue Eyes. How are you?"

"I'm fine now." I squeezed his hand.

"When did they say you could come back to classes? Do you remember your fall-semester classes?" He looked sad.

"No. I remember you, Mom, Dad, and Zach. I don't remember the classes." I studied his tan surfer skin and dark hair. His teeth were so white! Were they always so white? I felt so short next to him. Was he always a head taller?

"Do you remember Christmas break?"

"No. Should I? What happened?"

"Oh, nothing important." He kissed me softly on the lips. I felt nothing. His thick lips never parted and felt cold and dry, like my uncle kissing me hello.

Then Mom came outside and coughed a fake cough.

"Keoki, could I talk to you for a moment?" She pulled him away toward the garden and left me standing there.

The shadows changed the colors of the water. Haleiwa had been our home for, um, let me see. Haleiwa had been our home for, well, I don't remember. But it'll come back to me. It's been a long time. I know that. I breathed deeply the salted air and just knew with every pore of my being that I loved it here. I was truly part of this land, *Kama'aina.*

Our bungalow was a small two-bedroom, but I loved it, even though it was on the main highway that we just called Kam Highway. Even though we sometimes had huge cockroaches, and mom would have to call the exterminators, or the geckos would mess the counters as they held on to the ceiling, the atmosphere hugged me with unconditional love. I found day and night to be my friends equally; I never felt fear.

It was all Mom could afford after Dad left us. Then he wound up buying it for both of us.

I spotted the sun as it snuck behind the clouds and saw the light flickering on the two-story white Victorian next door. The Inn has been there for, um, well, like, forever, sometimes noisy, sometimes dead silent. Sometimes I swore it could breathe. I followed the light as it turned into shadows on the front of the lanai.

I didn't like the light shining down at me in the ocean. The color of the ocean is so beautiful when you look at it from land, blue-green with purple where the reefs are. In the water, though, it's a hazy blue. I got a chill thinking about it.

Keoki came back and grabbed my hand. He seemed different to me.

"Let's go to the beach."

"Okay." I said.

What happened on Christmas break?

***

Keoki was quiet at the beach. He used to go on and on about the waves, the height, and the curves. He said he always liked my curves better. I remember that. We snuggled real close.

"Do you want to talk about what happened?" he whispered in my ear.

I explained what dying was like and told him I wasn't scared of it anymore. Remembering was so hard, even my death. My mind sent a message to him, a hui hou kakou. Did he hear it?

He shook his head and stared out onto the waves rushing into the shore. "Your Mom said that you might never get back your full intellectual capacities."

Intellectual capacities. Hmm ... I didn't think I should ask him what that meant. But I didn't have something now that I once had. Before this, I used to be smart, real smart. Now, he might not want me.

"I'll get better." I smiled at him.

"Yeah."

We walked the beach and held hands. I didn't want to go into the water, and he understood. I watched him surf. He said the waves were rougher than usual.

I knew just how rough waves could be. They could be like horrible animals that hurt and kill people.

***

When I got home, Mom was sitting at the kitchen table crying. She stopped when she spotted me. I sat down next to her and glanced at the unread newspaper. The open windows let the red dirt from the Inn's roof blow onto the table. I remembered that Mom usually closed the windows, but today she didn't seem to care. The table got gritty, there were tourists' voices from the Inn's porch, and tears ran down her face.

"What's wrong?" I sat next to her.

"Oh dear," she stuttered. "You just started your last semester of college. We got to get you through your classes. I want you to get your degree and go to Berkeley for your masters, just like you planned, my poor, beautiful, brilliant baby."

"Is that gonna be hard?" I had no clue.

"We don't know." She paused and grabbed my hand. "We're not sure how long your brain was deprived of oxygen. But some of your surfer buddies saw you go down and think they got to you within a few minutes."

"It wasn't long. I remember being so tired, like I was getting sick. I didn't even hold my breath under water!" I got up and opened the refrigerator for a diet soda. "I remember drowning. I remember the lights, the chimes, and passing through the tunnel, oh yeah, and Tutu Styles! She had that strict look on her face and pointed for me to return through the tunnel. She said I had to help you. That's when I saw you crying and I came back."

"Well, I'm glad Mom sent you back to me."

"I think she was trying to tell me something. It seemed important."

"I'm fine, honey. I don't need your help. Zach and I are great, the store is holding its own, and wedding season is coming." She pulled the top section of the paper free from the rest. "Everything must seem so strange to you now."

Yes, it was strange. It was hard to keep things straight. Information got muddled like my thinking. I couldn't hold on to thoughts for long, and then childhood memories would drift in and out like a butterfly wandering among flowers. Life was misty, though—like the water after I was pulled under, when I was floating, very misty.

But all I could think about was ... "What's intellectual capacity?"

"It's what was affected by what happened, honey. You had a high ability to understand a lot of difficult stuff. "She shrugged her shoulders. "It really doesn't matter for what's important in life, and you remember that."

She stood and kissed me. "I love you, *a mau loa*, forever. "She squeezed my hand like when I was lying in the hospital bed.

"I love you too, Mom, a mau loa. "It didn't make me feel better, though.

"Lexi, do you remember our argument before you went surfing that day?"

"No. What did we argue about?"

"Oh, nothing important, honey. I was just wondering."

"Mom! What did we argue about before I went surfing?"

"You were very upset about something that happened at work."

"Work?" I worked somewhere? "Where did I work?"

"You worked with Zach on his farm. You were seeding his land for flowers and herbs and something happened. I don't know if you remember that you want to be an herbalist."

"What happened at the farm?"

"I don't know, really. You started to tell me, then stopped. Keoki works part-time with Zach when the surf shop is slow. Sometimes they even hang out together."

"What did we do there?"

"Keoki prepared the packets to place in the water for

the flowers, and you cut the flowers and took care of the hibiscus hedges, the ones used as barriers against the salt wind." She paused as I sipped my soda. "Lexi, you do know that Zach and I are serious, right? I'd say it's very serious."

"I didn't know it was that serious." I didn't remember anything about their relationship. Maybe I should force myself to think about them, about him? Did I like him?

"Well, it is. I don't think you really like him, but I love him."

***

The next day Mom came home with Zach. She had only dated two guys since Dad left her. Dad's a plastic surgeon who ran off with one of his nurses. He still paid Mom for my college education. I haven't spoken to him for ... jeez ... I don't know how long. I couldn't remember the argument they had when he left. He came home to pack up and say goodbye to me, and Mom came home unexpectedly early, like she used that sense that mom's have about things going on in their kid's lives. He packed, she screamed at the top of her lungs, and he left for the mainland. He kissed me and said he would call, but never did. Mom said he provided for both of us by buying the house. We didn't have to worry about the future.

Zach is handsome and wears a phony smile. Mom's prettier than he is handsome, though. I've got her long black hair and blue eyes. We almost look alike. But she's prettier. Her eyes are like a crystal blue. Mine are like my Dad's, sapphire blue. Keoki loves my blue eyes more than my long black hair or any other part of me, so he said.

***

"Hey, Cutie, how are you? You've been through hell and back." I hated being called Cutie by Zach. I remembered now that I didn't really like him. Mom was right about that.

"I'm getting better, Zach," I answered. Something felt different about him. I couldn't put my finger on it. Everybody seemed different to me, except Mom.

"Listen. Since you're a future herbalist, your mom asked me to help you with some of your science courses. What da ya think?" He smiled. His gray eyes stared down at me. He was as tall as Keoki, and Keoki was five-eleven, tall for most Japanese-Hawaiians. I was only five-two. Zach had gray sideburns and sandy-brown hair, and was shy with other people besides Mom and me. Keoki could talk to anyone. I loved Keoki so much. No keia la, no kiea lo, a mau loa—from this day, from this night, forever.

"Sure. You can tutor me." I really didn't want him to spend that much time with me, but I knew Mom would want me to say yes. She grinned.

"Great. We'll start tomorrow." He moseyed into my room without asking my permission. I looked at Mom and she nodded for me to follow him.

"I'll just need to take a look at your book." He grabbed my science book after he shuffled through some papers on my desk. Then he walked back to Mom in the kitchen. He kissed her. I heard him say, "I'll take a good look at this tonight, then ask Lexi some questions to assess where she's at." He shook his head slowly at her and stared into her eyes. They were having an unspoken conversation.

Mom kissed him.

I wanted to tell him off for just waltzing into my room and going through my papers. Keoki could help me with some of this, I thought. It would bring us closer if he could help me with my intellectual capacity. I looked the words up in the dictionary. Whew! How anybody could fill an intellectual capacity was beyond me!

"Keoki can help me, too. You both can."

"Sure, Honey. They both can help you. We know how you want to spend more time with Keoki."

My eyes got wet when Mom mentioned his name. I wanted to be with him that very second.

Nau ko 'u aloha. My love is yours.

He's gonna leave me for sure, I thought as my heart began to race. I'll read all night. He's coming over tomorrow after he gets done with work, and Mom will be at the florist shop. I looked up some big words and practiced them in sentences. Tomorrow I will say to Keoki: "I feel so lugubrious about dying."

***

It happened when I was watching TV. My brain went blank. I got dizzy. My head started to hurt. The pressure pushed both sides of my brain toward the middle. First there were blue stars, then gray, then dark. Tutu Styles flashed in the darkness and she was frowning. She shook her finger at me as if she disapproved of what I was doing. What do you want me to do, Tutu Styles? I implored her again in my mind: What do you want me to do?

Then blackness.

***

I felt myself being carried to bed, then I heard Zach's voice. "It's gonna be okay, Cutie."

My eyes fluttered.

"You had us going there for a minute," Zach said. "How're you feeling?"

"Fine." I did feel fine. I coughed and no water came in my mouth. I was very fine.

"Do you remember the paper you found?" he whispered softly. "Do you remember where you put it?" His mouth was close to my ear.

"No. What paper?" I whispered back.

"That's okay. I was checking to see what you remember. It was a gift list for your mother's birthday, that's all."

"Oh." I didn't remember taking any paper. Her birthday was still a couple of weeks from now, I thought.

My head stopped hurting and my brain crackled. Not like the crackling of the fish eating the coral, no; it was like the crackling of firewood in a fireplace. Like parts of my brain woke up and yawned, then stretched. I felt older.

Mom rushed in and Zach stood. She didn't have the chance to sit down, because I started to rise. "Mom! I remember the multiplication tables. I remember Earth Science and volcanoes and temperature and cloud formations and all the different rocks. I remember what Dad said when he left us, too! He said, 'Victoria, you suffocate me. I can't breathe with you around.' Is that right?"

Mom's shoulders slumped. I was so overjoyed at remembering that I didn't realize I hurt her feelings. "Oh, sorry, Mom." I eased back down on the bed.

"Yes, dear, that's what he said."

"What else do you remember?" Zach asked from behind Mom.

"Not much yet. Words. I remember what 'intellectual capacity' means!" I threw my feet over the side of the bed and jumped up.

Then I thought about the sentence I memorized for Keoki. Lugubrious about dying? Jesus! What was I thinking? I looked at Mom's questioning expression.

"I told you I wasn't dead long. I'm going to the surf shop to see Keoki. Okay if I borrow your car?"

My Mom clapped for joy. No tears rolled down her cheek. She grinned at me and said, "Sure, but maybe you should wait to see if this, well, will stay?" I could tell she resisted rushing toward me and giving me one of her heart hugs. "You sound older, too."

I hugged her hard, kissed her on the cheek, and grabbed my cell. "I'm going anyway. Thanks, Mom."

Mom looked concerned.

***

I backed the Nissan Cube out of the driveway, and the car seemed foreign to me. My instincts kicked into gear as I drove toward Haleiwa.

Something in my brain, the knowing me, the smart me, took control and whispered the directions.

I relaxed and reacquainted myself with Haleiwa's beauty. It captivated me, or should I say, recaptivated me. How could I ever want to leave here? I love it! Did I like working at Zach's? I didn't like him. I knew that for certain now. I think I might even detest him. Was that possible?

He and Mom were very serious.

Then everything went blank. My self stopped communicating. My breathing quickened and a headache grabbed my brain and squeezed. I pulled over. I had no aspirin. I didn't even bring any money, or my purse.

I controlled my breathing. My head still ached.

Suddenly, a vise grip clamped on my brain and I thought it would burst. I grabbed my head from both sides and pressed to hold it together. The pain was excruciating, and tears rolled down my face. I moaned. My hands shook so hard I couldn't pick up my cell phone to call 911.

Then the crackling sound came again, like firewood being consumed by flames. Each crackle, though, seemed to lessen the pain. As the pain subsided, I released the hold on my head. The tears stopped and I realized that I was gritting my teeth. My mouth hurt. My jaw hurt, but the pain in my head morphed into a dull pulsating ache.

My breathing regulated. I now knew the name and place of the surf shop.

I drove as slow as a gawking tourist while the past unfolded in waves of experiences.

I pulled over before I got to the shop's parking lot and devised a plan. I called as though I couldn't remember the exact address; I'd let him think not all the memories about him had returned.

"A hui hou kakou," I whispered to Keoki in my mind. "Till we meet again." My heart hurt. I wanted to cry, but kept my cool. So much had ended.

***

"Hey, Blue Eyes," Keoki said as I entered the shop. It all looked so familiar, but I glanced around in wonderment.

I remember hating the surf shop. Keoki loved the shop, and working part-time allowed him to talk story with the local surfers. It smelled like a rubber factory with all the rented flippers, wet suits, and snorkel gear lining the back of the shop, and the surfboards lining the side walls, and cheap clothes thrown in bins. I used to buy the ugly, tourist T-shirts to help support the store and Keoki working there.

Then I spotted Maria, my replacement, and the girl he cheated with.

"Let's walk outside." Keoki gently nudged me through

the door and toward my car. "Great news about you getting some of your memory back. Your mom called."

"Well, now that some of my memory is back, we can go back to planning our wedding." I reached up and pulled his face into mine and kissed him on the lips purposely.

"Lexi," he pulled my hands away from his face. "I don't know how to tell you this, but we broke up Christmas Day. Your mom said that the doctor recommended that we all let your memory come back naturally. Our breakup was for the best, and you even agreed. We're still friends. I just didn't have the heart to tell you while you were, well, not well. I'm sorry you don't remember the break-up."

I did remember the break-up, and it was nasty, hard and I wept for days. I found the gift you bought for Maria, a necklace with "*Ko aloha makamae e ipo.*"

"Sweetheart, you are so precious" was etched in a gold heart. I thought it was for me until I read the card that accompanied it. Asshole. You broke up with me!

My heart sank and drowned. I left as tears streamed down my cheeks and took off in the car. Only fifteen minutes ago, I was too tired to move, but now I was breathing more flames than Pele, goddess of the volcano.

Tutu Styles wanted me to warn Mom. Mom needed my help. Something was going on between Mom and Zack. But Zack loved Mom, didn't he. She most certainly loved him. Didn't she?

What was that unspoken communication between Mom and Zach in the kitchen? She did love him. They were very serious. He was looking for something on my desk. It was ... a license! Oh my God, it was a marriage license! Mom was now married to Zack? Was she really? Wait, maybe it wasn't a license. But they were married. Am I sure? How do I know that? Was that their secret conversation? Was that the silence that filled up the space between them and among us? Were they both looking for that piece of paper?

Yes. They were married.

Was that the fight we had before I drowned?

Didn't feel right.

Come on, come on, I know you're almost there. O, *no 'ono 'o*—think!

My head started to pound in uneven beats, like a drum. It was painful to think.

***

I threw the car keys onto the table and grabbed a diet soda from the fridge. Not only did my head start to spin from tiredness, but also my body felt like my skin wanted to crawl off of it. Exhausted, Zach flashed in my mind. He had carried an open can of soda and placed it on the kitchen counter that day, the drowning day. He was fooling around with something in the cabinet, then brought the can back to the table where I was sitting and placed it in front of me. "A peace offering," he had said, then left.

I walked over to the cabinet and opened it as if a clue would fall out on the counter for me to see. No such luck. The tall drinking glasses stood in their short rows like soldiers waiting for marching orders.

But before he had handed me the soda, he had yelled at me. "Why don't you want your mother to be happy? You're leaving anyway."

I was planning to go to Berkeley. They were married. I got tired after I drank the soda. Could he have put something in it? How could I think of such a thing? But, I did. I believed he could do that to me.

Mom walked in, dropped her keys on the counter next

to mine, smiled when she saw me, and came over to give me a kiss on the cheek.

I turned away. "You're married to Zach, aren't you, Mom?"

She plopped onto the chair and sighed. "Yeah, *male wahine*. I'm a married woman now. Happily married. The doctor—"

"I know. Keoki already told me!" I snapped at her. "You should have been the one to tell me, Mom, not Keoki."

My Mom's face turned grim.

"Is that what we were arguing about before I went surfing? You being married?"

"No, honey," she changed the subject. "I'm so sorry, honey, really, about Keoki. He broke your heart. He cheated on you. No wonder it took you so long to remember. He's going to quit the surf shop and work for Zach full time this summer. He's not planning to go off-island." She stood to give me a sideways hug and I pushed her away.

"What's going on? What's this about a paper on my desk? Tell me the truth, Mom. You might be in trouble. Tutu—"

"Your grandmother is dead, honey. No need to warn me about anything. I'm very happy, and Zach is a wonderful man."

"I think he may have put something in my soda to make me overtired and drown. He's not a wonderful man. I told you, his eyes say one thing and his mouth says another!"

"How dare you! How can you even think anything like that? I knew you would be jealous of him. You and I have been together for so long without anyone else, you can't stand seeing me with someone other than you. That's why you wouldn't sign over your share of the house."

"My share of the house?" What the heck was she talking about?

"Yes, when you turned eighteen, the house became half yours and half mine. Your dad thought that would be an equal way to provide for both of us."

Oh yeah, I remembered that.

"You said you might stay here, and you wanted to keep this as your home. But you can't afford it alone, and neither can I. We would have to sell all of it, or one of us would have to sell their share to the other."

"So let Zach come here and live when I leave. He can pay for half."

"You were thinking of maybe staying and going to U. of H. for your masters."

"Yeah?" That felt right. I loved it here. It was my home. *Hale aloha.*

"What were you going to do with the money if I gave you my half, and you sold the house when I left for school?"

"Buy Zach and me more land for his farm. There is land available right next to his three acres. You know how difficult it is for locals to order huge amounts of flowers for weddings from florists on-island. There are only one or two flower warehouses on Oahu. Zach is growing everything now. We could even ship to the mainland. We'd pay you back as the business grew."

"Doesn't he have any money?"

"All his money is in the land."

"He needed the land and he knew I didn't like him. So with me dead, he would have my share of the money from the house!"

"Don't say that! He loves you! I love you!"

"No he doesn't. We really don't like each other. Are

you sure he loves you?" I narrowed my eyes and spit out the words like a witch. She was going to sell me out for her husband, a man she married—behind my back no less.

She stormed out of the kitchen into her bedroom and slammed the door.

Tiredness overwhelmed me. Too many emotions. My eyes welled up again and my brain shut down. I lay on my bed.

Sleep lured me toward another world, a quiet world, the blue haze of the ocean. I was half-asleep and half-awake, breathing deeply, and then drowning, then dreaming.

Keoki was whispering to Zach at the wooden stand where the flowers were cut and wrapped for delivery. It was a cloudy day, and liquid sunshine fell softly on our faces. Zach and Keoki were so intent in conversation that they didn't see me nearby. Walking through the soft dirt of newly planted hibiscus bushes, they couldn't hear me either.

"After Vicky and I are married, I'll get her to sell the house. Then we'll have the money to grow and ship more of whatever we want. I already have buyers. You can work part of the business. We'll start shipping next spring. As long as we can keep the goddamn agriculture department off the land, which shouldn't be too difficult, we'll be fine. I've always had a great relationship with them. They'll never suspect."

The fish at the coral were whispering. I was floating. So tired. So sleepy.

He didn't sound as though he loved Mom.

Anxiety befuddled my thinking.

I must have gone home and started to confront her. I

wonder what she said. Did I hurt her feelings? Did she hurt mine? We'd had many a battle, but none ever left scars.

Somewhere between fish nibbling and humans whispering, I fell asleep. My last thoughts included plans.

***

I heard Zach's car approach as I sat with Maxine Hunter, a contract-law teacher from the University of Hawaii. I decided to continue my education there and invited Ms. Hunter over for coffee. I rattled off the whole story over the phone that morning after placing all my thoughts in a succinct order, a lot of the story she already knew through the coconut express. The Hawaiian wind carried the story to the four corners of Oahu, and to no one's surprise.

She had asked me to locate the mysterious paper, probably a contract, so she could review everything. Mom was working at the florist shop, so I knew I had plenty of time. I searched throughout the house, starting in Mom's room. I even combed through her private box of pictures and flower awards. Then I moved to the kitchen and scoured every nook and cranny. I moved to the screened-in porch, although not much could survive the dampness and heat, and some of the insects that visited. Even the stealthy whicker slumped with wear. I finally found it between pictures in my own photo album under my bed. It was under a picture of me snuggling with Dad on the lanai, holding hands, and making faces at Mom.

I loved dad so much at that moment, and wished he hadn't left us.

Then, I shivered as I studied my signature. I had signed the contract giving away my half of the house to Mom and Zach.

What was I thinking? I know I didn't want to do that.

She made a few phone calls from her cell as I made coffee. She also called the Department of Agriculture, a tough-minded crew of strict agents that protected our land. *Malama aina*. They would leave no stone unturned, no plant unidentified, and no crop uncounted. Zach's farm would be examined for anything illegal, or crops that were allowed in limited quantities, like tobacco. As I poured the Kona coffee, I suggested to Ms. Hunter that maybe the lab was looking for the wrong chemicals when they did my tests, after I drowned. She said she would have the doctor recheck all the results before she turned the information over to the police. She wanted to move with caution, she said, and judiciously.

Zach was screwed. So was Keoki. Even though I couldn't prove it, I believed Zach tried to kill me.

Tutu Styles told me. "Go back, help your mother. She needs you."

Maybe he was planning to kill her, too?

Zach's fake smile melted when he saw Ms. Hunter. He glanced at both of us several times trying to buy time to think.

"I'm a lawyer, and my name is Maxine Hunter, and I have been hired by Ms. Lexi Evans to represent her in the case of an attempted illegal, forced sale of this house. She has also placed a formal complaint with the Department of Agriculture whose agents are searching your property." She looked at her watch, "As we speak."

"You bitch!" Zach yelled at me. His eyes and his words finally matched. "Your mother will be heartbroken! Do you have any idea what this will do to her, you selfish bitch!"

"Yeah, she'll be heartbroken about you. She doesn't

know what you're growing on your farm. She doesn't know what you and Keoki had planned when you got her to sell this house and buy more land for you."

He pointed an angry finger at Ms. Hunter. "I'm surprised you're fooled by this ... this ... liar! I'll get the best damn lawyer in Hawaii."

"I'm sure you will." Ms. Hunter grinned. "Good luck with that. A hui hou kakou."

Murder
Interrupted Me

I have waited for this day forever. Well, yeah, at least it seems that way. Like eons, man.

My wife rarely gives me time I can call my own. I'd say seconds, but that would be too long. I'd say nanoseconds, but you know what? The shit I take makes time meaningless. Just like my life is meaningless to my old lady.

How I've longed for this day! To finally unwind, fish, do drugs in the open air, and most important, be alone. Oh yeah. I love being alone. I love alone. Sitting here next to the stream, fishing, tripping, toking, just me, myself, and I. Heaven! Though on this shit, you're never really alone.

Still, you know what I mean. Without the bitch hounding, hounding me—"Mow the lawn!" "Clean the garage!" "Fix the leaky faucet!"—I get to see the deep, rippling stream yanking at my feet, like it wants to grab them. I get to hear the rushing water and the air rustling through the long soft grass, like fingers fluffing hair, but louder.

Hell, I get to focus on one blade of grass, become it and feel the heartbeat of nature pounding in my chest.

Wow, am I buzzing. Shoulda taken a little less.

Then again, maybe not. I mean, I'm sitting on the bank and hanging over it in the sky. I scan Earth through my telescopic vision, courtesy of my best girlfriend Mary Jane, and Ice, cold blue and fast, and two tasty blotters of acid, purple Popeyes painted on them. Can you feel it too? Are you getting a contact high? Oh, man, it's the most wonderful place to be in the universe, and I mean the whole wide world, from Spain to Austral ... ya ... Aus ... Oz! Yeah, man, that way big continent in ... like ... the ocean. The ocean. Ocean big. All that water. This water, in this stream, eventually finding its way to that water, in that ocean.

Where was I?

Oh, yeah, puffing, puffing, puffing along with Mary Jane. Yeah. Puff the plastic decoy lived by the stream and frolicked in a—

"What the hell are you doing!"

Hm. Is that noise inside or outside my head? Has to be inside, seeing as how my head is the universe.

I turn around, which takes a really long time, but finally I look and I see ... boots. Workman's boots. I think. I mean, the shape I'm in, I can't be sure. Because they also resemble puppies, with big noses in front and all the little eyes making two big eyes, though they need floppy ears hanging over each side, maybe skimming the ground. If one puppy went to bite the other puppy's ear, would the big workman trip and fall on his face? Too funny.

"What are you laughing at? This is my land and you're trespassing. I'll give you ten seconds to leave. Then I'm calling the police."

Ten seconds? How long is that? Oh. Yeah. About as

long as my wife gives me to think about what I want to do and not what she wants me to do. Oh Wow! That cloud over his shoulder. Is it the face of a woman screaming? Her mouth is getting wider and wider and wider. She must be screaming louder. There isn't a day go by that I don't hear screaming. My wife screaming how unhappy she is. Screaming like the cloud.

Man, this dude is big. Towering over me. Should probably get up and talk to him, face to face, although I can't make out his face. Where is his face? Sun's too bright!

The puppies are glaring at me. The two metal eyes and the long nose held together by string. No, no, rope. No, no, shoelaces, no, rope, no, string. The sole is separating and mouth is opening, ready to scream at me. Like the cloud. The other puppy is looking on.

"Bite that other puppy's ear," I say to the quiet one.

"You're fuckin' stoned!" The faceless voice yells down at me. "You're out-of-it. Can you even think straight? You were smoking pot, weren't you? I know you were."

"This is California. Stoned is okay. I have my medical card." I shove my hand into my pocket and search for the card. Not there. Other pocket. I go to the other pocket and slowly pull it out. "Look."

"You're not just stoned! You on other drugs? Do you even know where you are?"

"Shoot, yeah. Hell, yeah. South Fork somewhere, Folsom Lake, Folsom, Folsom ... prisons and damns. Ha! Damn prisons ... ha ... ha ... ha." I start singing, "I walk the line, ha ... ha ... ha. Me and Johnny."

"I'm trying to help you stay out of prison! You're trespassing. You better get out of here, right now."

"Right this nanosecond?" I laugh.

The screaming cloud distorts. The mouth separates and disappears.

"That's your Celica parked right out there on the road, isn't it?" He points to the road behind me.

"Yep."

"For the last time and for your own good, I'm telling you to leave. Otherwise, you're going to be in big trouble."

"Okay." The puppies are smiling at me now. Quiet puppies. Good puppies.

"Okay? Okay what? Get up and leave!"

"Okay, you're telling me, for the last ... Hmm ... "

The one puppy opens its mouth. "That's it! I'm calling the cops."

The puppy's a riot.

"It's not funny. Get up!"

"Okay, puppy, I'm moving." I figure I should anyway. The cops and all. I bend my legs and push. "I'm moving, see? You're as mad as my wife on Saturday morning."

"Huh?"

"She gives me a big fuckin' list of chores. No fishing. Just yelling. No talking like we used to. No asking. Big list to keep me away. Now I'm away."

He shakes his head.

I get up. I'm up. I watch the current trying to grab my feet. I stomp on it. It spits at me.

"So, you're not too fucked up to move. Good. Now go."

I look and the huge guy without a face is now wearing bottle-thick glasses, staring at me. The better to see you with, my dear? The big brown eyes, the color of dead leaves, blink. Those glasses, I think, like microscopes.

"Go ahead. Call the cops," I say as I stumble toward the

stream. "But I gotta move this log. Can't fish with this log in the way."

"What log? What fish?"

I glance back at the guy. Now he doesn't seem that big. He's not reaching for his cell phone. He's not moving at all. At least, I don't think he is. But the puppies are staring down the road, like they hear something coming. And his hands have turned into claws, big rounded hooks that could tear me apart.

Wow. Maybe I shouldn't have had that second acid blotter.

Jesus, that's a big log for such a small stream. Seems stuck. If I move it, I'll bet there's a big-ass fish lurking underneath.

Ah, fishing! Finally. How long has it been since I went fishing? Can't even begin to remember. At least since I got married. She was so nice before that. But then she—

Fuck it! Just Fish! See the water separate, no flapping. Listen to your breathing like the current. Smell the dirt. Feel the freedom as you reel it in.

"Rick, you gotta get the fuck out of here now!" he yells. "Otherwise, it'll be too late. Leave now!"

Too late? For what? Dinner? To ride the sky? And how does this guy know my name?

He's still talking. At least, his mouth is moving. But now I can see through him. Like the dirt, grassy shit, yeah, right through him.

And look. The log is moving toward me. I see the trees. Breeze smells funny now. I feel the water at my feet. I hear wheels on gravel.

The sun's rays tap the water, causing little ringlets to appear next to one another. The fish bites. Lucky me. My little fly decoy caught a big-ass fish right near the log.

"Run!" he screams. "Run now! Right now!" He slowly rises from the earth, like a slow-moving helium balloon, the puppies reaching my knees, then my shoulders and finally my face. They stare at me, their ears limp, their eyes dead. One of them opens its mouth to say, "I tried to warn you, Rick. I tried. That's all a survival instinct can do. But you wouldn't listen. You're too fucked up to know it's me, your survival instinct. Run!"

Something stirs deep inside me. My stomach hurts. That's all a survival instinct can do? Not a real guy, a survival instinct? But then I laugh it off. Ha ha! Funny, those puppies.

A pointed triangle pops out of the water, a small pointed triangle, with nostrils.

This is very strange. Fish don't have nostrils, do they?

Strong shit. Woo.

The current's really ripping. It will help pull in the fish.

Oh, there's the mouth, open wide like in a circle. A car door slams behind me. I turn and see flashing lights and a man in uniform talking into a box that crackles. Another man holds a photo.

I like my puppies better.

"He's here."

True enough. I am here.

A man walks over to the edge of the stream and looks at a photo in his hand. "Yep, that's her."

Yeah, big-mouth bass, I think. On the log? No.

The man with the photo looks at me and says, "You're under arrest for the murder of your wife."

Someone else grabs me and pulls my arms behind my back.

"I am? No, man, I was just fishing."

"Fishing? You don't even have a fishing rod!"

Love Shack

The love shack is a little old place
Where we can get together.
Love shack, baby—
Love shack.
That's where it's at.
—B-52's

Makonu saw himself as an easygoing guy, even though he held everything in. Maybe this weekend he would get the chance to dive at Ewa Beach, or fish, or just "talk story" with his Nanakuli friends in his garage, on old couches facing his neighbor's rusted-out car and Sovereignty sign, quenching the midday heat with beer. Becca's list was long, and he needed to get some work done around his yard.

He stepped outside his small two-bedroom home and ambled down the short driveway to the mailbox. He scanned the houses to his right and left, identical in every way except color and care. He yanked down the rusted lid and grabbed the mail, thumbed through it, and paused to look at two life-insurance bills he'd paid quarterly for the last thirty-seven years.

"Damn it to hell," he grumbled. "These again? Every time I turn around I'm paying another life-insurance policy. And for what? So Becca can enjoy the rest of her life without me, after all the crap I've put up with for all these years?"

He stared at the envelope and wondered if he might stop paying the premium on his own policy. After all, she'd get the house, her teacher's pension, and his retirement benefit from the Electrical Workers union. Then he wondered about her policy, since she'd almost certainly outlive him, and what good would it do either of them then?

Smacking the pile of bills against his palm, he glanced up at the morning sun beating down on him with the burning promise that every day would remain the same. No rainbows. Too warm on this side of the Island.

He sighed, and his shoulders slumped. Thirty-seven years married to Becca, and only five of them in marital bliss. If he'd only known then what he knew now. "Damn it to hell," he repeated once again.

It's been pure torture since he ended his business—his bones had been hurting from all the knee-bending, pulling electric wires from spools, and taking crap from construction foremen, most of them Haoles, and transient workers from other islands or the mainland. But, Becca had more demands than management and the Haoles combined, maybe even worse than his staff sergeant in the Army, a Jawaiian from up island near Haleiwa.

Makonu had killed in Vietnam, but that was war, and what he was doing in the mainland's war, he'd never knew. He knew it was useless.

And he knew he could never hurt Becca, not in his wildest fantasy. Never. Or could he? Could doing her in be considered anything but murder? No, it couldn't. Period.

At least he could go to their cabin near the Ko'olau Mountain Range, and fish not too far from Chinaman's Hat, as often as he liked, now that he was no longer working. He could hike and do a little fishing and diving off the boat of his old army buddy Rocco, when they were at their cabins at the same time. But most importantly, he could read the latest boating magazines and dream about buying his own boat, his forever dream. A dream where he drifted slowly on the ocean, reading his history books, listening to slack-key guitar solos, smelling the salt air, and staring at the wandering clouds, and the Ko'olau range with it's different shades of green and slippery coast. But as Becca reminded him often: "Your head is always in the clouds."

He easily clicked open the gated door, and moseyed into the small gold-painted living room where his old dark-green recliner sat next to a worn brown-leather couch that Becca's sister had given them two years earlier. Across from the furniture, between two narrow double-hung windows, a state-of-the-art 52-inch high-definition 3D TV hung on the wall above his stuffed bookshelf and next to his weights. A small dining room adjoined a big updated kitchen that cost them a bundle. If only Becca hadn't given up cooking, he might have enjoyed it more.

"Did you get the mail?" Becca called from the second bedroom that she converted into her sewing area. If only she had sewn one item of anything for him, he thought, he wouldn't have minded donating his office to her.

"Yeah, only junk and the life-insurance bills."

"What do you mean junk? Did my Macy's catalog

come? Did my knitting magazine arrive? Was my bingo club newsletter in there?"

"Nope. Sorry. But your hiking and runners world came," he snickered.

"Not funny, Makonu. You know I can't do any of that with my limp. You're being nasty. Just because you lift weights and walk and jog doesn't mean I can."

Me nasty? You didn't let your limp stop you from making mad passionate love at the love shack when we met, and for the first years of our marriage.

"I'm gonna read the paper, Becca," he said as he pulled the front section from the Honolulu Star-Advertiser. "See what's happening in the world."

"Fine. I'm going out with Sandy and grab some breakfast. I'll see you later."

"I thought you wanted to take a ride today, maybe go down Kailua way."

"No. I told you. You have to finish cleaning the garage, and then you said you'd get rid of the old paint cans in the back yard. The sun is hot this time of year."

"Well, I'll do that later, okay?"

"Later? It's always later with you!"

"Hmm, better than not at all, Becca."

"Don't start. I do enough around this house. I keep this place spotless! You know that."

"Yeah, I know." He thought, how could I not? You remind me of it three times a day. "Just go." He waved a dismissal hand at her, and sat on the recliner and skimmed the front page. Sovereignty was always a big issue. Will we, the Hawaiian nation, finally be free?

"Don't forget to pay the bills!" she yelled as she slammed the back screen door for effect, reminding him that he wasn't as successful as Sandy's husband, the accountant, though they were certainly comfortable enough. Makonu scanned the headlines on the second page, but his mind drifted away as his eyes gazed at words.

Becca had been a dark-hair beauty with caramel eyes. Being the same age and height fit him perfectly, and her limp from childhood Polio never stopped her from doing anything; it gathered her lots of pity that she often lapped up like a thirsty puppy. She would sometimes even exaggerate the limp, but not often.

Clever should have been her middle name.

It did earn them a handicap-parking permit, worth its weight in gold, especially during tourist season. Also, he noticed that her limp was getting a bit worse and, although she could eat anything and not gain weight, and she had an ageless kind of beauty, she was looking pale and drawn at fifty-nine. Her feisty disposition, added by a chip on her shoulder, had waned.

What people saw second was her angelic, kind, giving, and hard-working side. She could be soft-spoken and sweet. Many of her loving traits blossomed in the company of others, but not with him. She was disappointed in her husband. He was disappointed in their marriage.

They called the cabin the "love shack," long before the song of that name became famous—although they could have composed the lyrics. Her mother's family had owned it for generations, and rented it to him thirty-six years ago so he could study for his electrician's license. However, Becca's mother forgot she'd promised the cabin to Becca that same week, as a getaway from job searching. He was hunched over his textbooks when she walked in the door. Makonu couldn't believe his good luck. It felt like destiny.

And that night, fireworks exploded, thunderous waves

hit boulders jetting into the ocean as they got to know each other.

The total collapse of rational thinking was his demise.

They married within the year, and Makonu spent every penny he'd saved from his Army pay to buy the love shack as their own getaway. He hoped the god, Kamapua'a, would protect the cabin and the moist land near the mountain. They found jobs in Honolulu and, within five years, settled into a routine he would have never imagined to be so boring. Worse, Becca turned from his wounded angel of light to a critical mockingbird, squawking at him day and night.

The newspaper drifted toward Makonu's lap as he fell into a deep sleep. In his dream, he and Becca were fairy-tale-people, young and beautiful, and the fairy-tale cottage resembled Hansel and Gretel's house, but with hundred dollar bills as the outside covering. Makonu plucked a hundred-dollar bill and gave it to his dark-haired beauty to buy herself golden slippers in town. After Becca left the cottage and skipped down a 14K goldbrick road, Makonu drove to his new boat and skippered it out on the water. He eased onto the plush captain's chair and threw out a fishing line without bait or direction or a care as to catching a fish. A tug on his line caught his attention. A soft, angelic voice called his name.

"Makonu, I have something to tell you," it sung in his mother's voice. "It's important, so listen to me."

He stuck his head out over the deck and studied the water. A mermaid appeared. She looked like his mother with fins and a tail–not a pretty sight. "Makonu, you've been a good husband, and would have been a good father, if that you-know-who didn't ruin your life, and decide not to have children. Sure your business did not bring much, but the times were hard on the island. The economy dropped. Sure, you had to take a little money out of the house. But you have the insurance policy. Think freedom. Maybe she could have a little accident. A makana for you."

The vividness of the dream alarmed him, and its message disturbed him. He needed to examine the possible reality of his fantasy. He had killed men in the army, but that was self-defense. Think freedom, his mom had said, like Pele, the goddess of the volcano, when she entered the Ko'olau mountains. His mother was like his fairy godmother, and had come from heaven to visit. But he knew he could never hurt Becca, not in his wildest nightmare. Never. Could he? Could killing her be considered self-defense? No, it couldn't. Period.

Be not far from me;
For trouble is near;
For there is none to help.
—Psalm 22:11

"Listen, Becca." Makonu slid a slice of sausage pizza onto his paper plate leaving a greasy trail. "I know I've been hard to live with these last few days, and I'm sorry." He bit into the slice and a strand of the mozzarella cheese hung onto the slice as he placed it back on his plate. He twirled the strand around his finger, popped it in his mouth, and chewed.

"Yeah, you have been. I get the impression you don't even like me any more."

He finished chewing and studied her caramel eyes. "Now that I'm retired, we need to renew our relationship. I still love you, and I'd like to go back in time and remember what it was we loved about each other, yeah? Aloha au ia 'oe. I really do. I've been thinking we should go back to the love shack and be together—talk, play cards, read books to each other, and make love. What do you think? Do you think we can renew our relationship, and have a chance at happiness together? Because if you don't, it might be time to split. Neither of us wants to go into life's last phase feeling like we do now."

Becca's eyes bulged and she gulped. "Divorce? You gotta be kidding me! We can't afford a divorce."

"Sure we can. We could sell the house. The economy has come back, people are visiting, and there's more work. We'd get a lot of money, especially with the new kitchen. Subtract the debt and add the money from the redeemable insurance policy, and we'd wind up with close to two hundred thousand apiece. But that's not the point, Becca. Either we renew our marriage or we can't afford not to get a divorce." He picked up his slice and took another bite, watching her eyes move in thought.

She was considering the divorce, he could tell. He expected her to ask for alimony within the minute.

He was feeling free already.

"No, I couldn't see myself alone or with anyone else. I love you, Makonu, I do. Aloha au ia 'oe. You're right. Let's go to the cabin and work on the relationship. You have been so good to me and I've, well, I don't want to lose you."

Damn it, anyway!

***

The ride to the cabin proved to be more fun than Makonu had anticipated. Becca made lunch and packed snacks, his favorite Hawaiian Kettle chips and mozzarella sticks, with his pork sandwich, and enlivened the drive with stories from their past. He wished he thought of threatening divorce sooner!

When they passed Rocco's cabin, next to theirs, Rocco was sitting on his top step. He was expecting Makonu, but when he got up and approached the car, Rocco gawked at Becca, who hadn't been to the cabin in years. Makonu knew that Rocco didn't care for Becca, but because Makonu had been his buddy since the army, and had saved his life during the second Battle of Saigon, he would always be cordial to her. Becca waved back, and added a smile.

The brown cabin, with the hand-written Love Shack sign over the door, rested placidly on a small, even plot that Rocco kept cut. Thick brush outlined the property, threatening to overwhelm the small cabin. Becca stepped in and dropped her suitcase. Makonu followed her and laid his duffle bag on a dinette chair.

"It's been awhile since you've been here," Makonu said to Becca.

"Yeah, it looks good. The knotty pine paneling has held up well. It didn't turn yellow."

"I varnished it last year."

"Is that a new rug on the floor? I like the design."

"Last year, too. Right when I retired, I bought the rug and varnished the paneling and bought a new, well, used kitchen table and four chairs, and a new bed cover and sheets." He expected her to berate him for spending the money, then not telling her.

"Wow, I had no idea so much had changed." She strolled around the room and studied it as if for the first time. "Good job."

"Well, it's been, what, three years since you've come here with me?"

"Yep, three years." She moseyed up to the window. "You took down the curtains I made?"

"Yeah, moths got to them."

They could hear the gecko's *toc, toc, toc* from somewhere on the cabin.

"I'll just have to make new ones. Yep, I'll spruce up the place. You'll love it."

Makonu was shocked. "You'll really make curtains for the cabin?" She hadn't even darned any holes in his socks in over ten years! "That would be great, honey!"

They settled in the cabin. Becca unpacked her suitcase, readied some hamburgers, put away the kitchen supplies, and slipped on hiking boots. "Do you want to go for a walk down the path a bit. It's too steep to go for a real hike."

"You want to go for a hike?" Makonu asked in surprise.

"Well, a short one. I'm not in the shape you are. But the Fan Palms—ho'onani. I forgot how beautiful the Ohia trees are, too."

Makonu hugged her. "Mahalo, Becca. This is wonderful! And I saw a Koa butterfly on a Manaki scrub! I'll show you where."

Becca held him tight, then kissed him tenderly.

Monkonu's heart jogged with excitement as anticipation ran through his veins. What a kiss!

"It'll be good to stretch our legs and I'd like to see the old path."

"The one near the steep ridgeline?"

"Yeah, near the gully."

"Okay, so we'll go for a short walk. I'll show you the Manaki bush."

"Sure." She grabbed her sweater off the hook near the front door. "There's a chill up here."

"New?" Makonu asked.

"Yes! I can't believe you noticed. I just got it at a sale with Sandy. It's got big pockets, and it's light, but warm."

"Looks nice on you." Makonu liked her in beige. Brought out the color of her hair and eyes.

"I don't remember that denim jacket, either."

"I keep it here," Makonu said, showing her the lining. "For the cool clear nights under the stars."

"Remember that poem: 'The woods are lovely, dark and deep, but we have miles to go before we sleep,'?" Becca asked as they stepped onto the path toward the dimly lit forest.

"Yeah, Robert Frost," Makonu answered. "Snow in his poem, but never here."

"Yeah, but that's what these woods remind me of, that poem. They're not as thick, but ... I'll follow you," she added.

"No, ladies first," he waved her in front of him.

"No, I don't know where I'm going. You first."

They set out, Makonu in the lead, Becca following closely behind. Twigs crackled and the path grew thin. Thorny weeds slowed their pace and thick brush converged from both sides.

"Are we lost?" Becca sounded nervous.

"No, the ridgeline is right over there. Watch your step. We'll go slow." He could also see a light on over the back door of Rocco's cabin through the trees. As Makonu turned to proceed, he felt an intense sharp stabbing pain under his shoulder blade and something warm and wet drip down his back. He let out a roar of pain. "What the–"

He spun around to see Becca holding his carving knife from the kitchen. "What are you doing?" he yelled as she lunged at him, knife pointed at his stomach.

He raised his hands and managed to shove her toward

the gully as the blade ripped through the jacket just missing his stomach.

Becca stumbled and fell backward.

Makonu dropped to his knees, reached over, gripped her arm, and ripped the knife from her hand. "You're trying to kill me!" he gasped.

"That's right!" she shouted, scrambling to her feet. "I hate you, our home, and especially this cabin. I call it the Hate Shack now! Sandy laughs every time I say it!" She reached into her pocket and pulled out a second blade, a short paring knife, and raised the knife to plunge it into him.

A shot rang out from the woods.

Becca grunted and fell. Her mouth opened in surprise, and within a few seconds, her eyes closed for the last time.

Rocco helped Makonu to his feet. "You all right, buddy? Here, let's take off this jacket and see where she got you."

Makonu winced as Rocco pulled the sleeve off his arm.

"Jesus, can you believe the balls on her, Makonu? Two knives! It's almost like she'd been in the infantry."

"She really had me fooled. I actually thought she'd changed after the threat of divorce. Aloha for covering my back."

I told you when you retired you should have left her, but you didn't listen."

"How bad is it, Rocco?"

"You'll live," Rocco said, inspecting the knife wound through Makonu's torn shirt. "Lucky you had that jacket on."

"I've got half a mind to dump her into the gully and let the wild pigs and whatever else find her."

Both men stared into the vast hole.

"Nah. We need to leave her right where she is and go call the police. Open and shut case of self defense."

"I can't believe she really tried to kill me! You just saved my life, Rocco!" He stared at the body stunned. "I'm in shock. Wow, mahalo, buddy."

"Yeah, now we're even. C'mon. Let's go get you patched up. Then we'll take down that stupid Love Shack sign from over your door."

LA Car

Greg and Sandy Johnson spread their pale blue blanket on the crowded sands of Venice Beach, near the new restaurant named LA Car.

Sandy eased down on the blanket and placed her *Elle* and *Cosmo* magazines next to her. "What a gray day. Look at those clouds. Do you think it's going to rain?" Her tan beach bag sagged, exposing maps, *Car* Magazine, a bag of potato chips, a small umbrella, and a hat.

Greg plopped down and scanned the skies. "Like that old song says, it never rains in California. You didn't have to bring an umbrella. Those aren't storm clouds. It's smog." He sniffed and smiled.

Sandy shed the black-silk bathing-suit cover-up, and dug into the bag for suntan lotion. She slathered her thin arms, long legs, and flat stomach.

Greg leaned back on his elbows. "Can you hand me the car magazine, honey?"

Sandy wondered if Greg could allow himself to sit still for one hour, or thirty minutes, or even fifteen. This vacation was meant to strengthen their strained relationship, and she already had doubts. "I heard that sigh. You promised you'd relax, not feel anxious, and not hunt for possible clues to a crime scene," she lifted both hands from her sides, shook her shoulders, and announced, "at scenic Venice Beach, home of power-lifting men and Miss Universe women." She chuckled.

"Greg flexed his well-defined bicep. Hey, at least we're not fat tourists from Harrisburg. We're thin tourist from Harrisburg. And you, doll, fit right in, with those gorgeous hazel eyes, long hair, long legs, perfect, uh, perfect bod."

"Yeah. I don't see any redheads here, though. Mostly bleached blondes." She pulled a floppy wide-brim hat out of the bag and placed it on her head. "Bet they don't have as many freckles as I do, either. Think we'll see any movie stars?"

"Maybe Jaws."

"Not funny."

"Sandy?" Greg picked up the magazine, then looked right at her.

"Yeah?" Sandy said, detecting a change in his voice.

He finger-combed his wavy brown hair, gazed out to sea, cleared his throat, then met her eyes. "I've been thinking, and you're right. Being a private investigator has taken over my life. I've excluded you. I was wrong to take that job during your brother's wedding and leave as they were exchanging vows."

"Ya think? How could you not turn your phone off, especially with that damn barking-dog ring? Everyone in the room was staring at us, even the bride and groom. It was horrible!"

"And I was wrong to take your camera when I came back to the reception, just because I dropped mine chasing that blackmailer. I know how important that wedding was and how you wanted the pictures."

"And what about that time at my mother's birthday party?"

"Please, I'm sorry. I promise I will never take off with her car again. I won't take off with anyone's property again."

"You've heard this before, Greg, but we have trust issues. I can't trust that you're telling me the truth about where you're going and what you're doing. Mom would have given you the keys to her car. All you had to do was ask."

Greg nodded.

She eyed Greg, then frowned. "It's not just about the trust, either, you know. You're never around. When you're not busy with work, you hang out at the gym with your cop buddies, or go look at some rare car, or hang out at the bar. And none of this is new to you."

"I know, I know." Greg nodded. "But today starts with a new beginning. I can't lose you. I love you."

"As you would say, I need proof, Greg. I need *evidence* that you're really going to change this time. We've been married for ten years. In two years, I'll be forty. I'm not spending my golden years with a man I can't depend on. My job is a big enough hassle."

"I got it, honey. I'm with you on this. I really *hear* you. That's why I planned this vacation. I get points for that, don't I?"

"Yep."

"Big points or little points?"

"Medium points."

"This is our time together. I won't even answer my phone unless it's family."

Sandy loved Greg, but lived in a constant state of frustration, worry, and exasperation. Being an emergency-room nurse supplied her with enough of all three. "We'll see."

"Well, I gotta start somewhere. And wait till you see what I have planned for you tomorrow, and it's not even your birthday. This will be one of our best vacations. You'll see."

"Really?" Sandy smiled. "What?"

A whirring sound interrupted them. It grew louder and louder and they both looked toward the water, then to either side of them.

"Where is that coming from?" Sandy asked.

From behind them came a voice. "Hello. I'm from LA Car restaurant. May I take your drink order?

Sandy turned to see a long remote-controlled wagon.

"Holy shit! That's a Woodie!" Greg exclaimed as he studied an old station wagon.

"A what?"

"A Woodie station wagon. A Woodie is a car body style, mainly station wagons, where the rear bodywork is constructed of a wood framework." He pointed to the oak inlays. "With inlay panels of wood. It's a nineteen forty-six! What a beauty. I heard they had a lot of old cars like this on the road in California. It must be the weather." Greg reached out to touch the small-scale purple replica.

"Please don't touch me," the car said. "It's inappropriate."

Sandy chuckled. She thought the voice was coming from the front grille. "How do you work?" She yelled as if the car was deaf.

"You give me your order. When I return to the bar, my co-worker, the bartender—who makes the best cocktails in Venice and is adorable to boot—prepares your drinks, with covers to insure no spillage. He places the drinks through my retractable roof into holders. Then I deliver the drinks to you. Would you like to open a tab or pay as you go?"

Incredible, Sandy thought. Absolutely amazing. Only in California. "How do we pay?" She yelled at the car again.

"You swipe your credit card along my front bumper. But if you're ordering, first, I'll need to see your license. Hold it in front of my windshield."

Greg removed his license and credit card from the back pocket of his jean shorts.

"Do you think you should, Greg? If they take a picture, they could sell it."

"Now you're sounding like me. I'm sure it's okay." He pressed his license against the windshield and a light scanned it. "They thought of everything."

"Are you staying at a nearby hotel?" the car inquired.

"The Sea Colony Condos."

Greg went to swipe his card.

"Not yet, please. You pay when you receive the drinks. May I take your order?"

They both ordered margaritas.

"I will return shortly."

The machine whirred away, the big tires kicking sand onto their blanket.

Greg watched the station wagon travel to the restaurant about a hundred feet away. "I want one of those!" The car drove onto a patio, past colored plastic chairs and tables with matching unopened umbrellas, and through two open glass doors. As the Woodie left his sight, another remote-controlled car rolled out of LA Car.

"Oh, my God!" Greg yelled. "It's an antique Mercedes Gull Wing! The doors open upward, not outward. I bet that's where they place the drinks. I once had a copy of the designs for that car. I can't believe I sold them."

"So much for having a serious conversation," Sandy said, then smiled. Watching Greg's reactions delighted her. Cars were Greg's hobby, one that sometimes kept him home and in the garage.

"Next drink, we want the Mercedes! What a great gimmick. I'm sure people drink more just to watch the cars."

"What makes me think you'll be one of those people?"

"I can't wait to see what comes out next. If we buy drinks from all the models, you might have to carry me home."

Sandy watched the people going into the restaurant. Two official-looking men in jackets and ties caught her interest. Suits in California, she thought, and at the beach? Business meeting? Law enforcement?

The Woodie returned. The roof opened and four rounded spaces for drinks appeared, two holding lidded plastic drink cups. Greg slipped both drinks from their holders and handed one to Sandy. "Wow, these are actually cold."

The bill was inserted in the back pouch of the front passenger seat.

"Cash or credit card?" the car asked.

"Credit."

"Please swipe your credit card through my front bumper."

Greg did as he was told, smiling the whole time. "Oh man, I'm taking a picture of this. The guys won't believe it."

Two receipts popped up through the top of the driver's seat.

"Please sign the merchant's copy and take your customer receipt."

Greg snatched both, looked at them. "I don't have ..."

A pen shot out of the tailpipe. "Please return the pen after you sign."

"Someone has a sick sense of humor," Greg said as he signed the restaurant's copy.

"Thank you. Please place the signed copy in the glove compartment and close it."

"Thank you!" the Woodie repeated. It actually sounded grateful for the business as the glove compartment door closed.

Greg whipped out his iPhone and snapped a picture of the car. "There, I just sent the picture to the boys back in Harrisburg. It'll be around the police department before we finish our drinks."

The station wagon turned toward the patio and Sandy handed Greg his drink.

"Wait!" Greg yelled after it.

The station wagon stopped and backed up. "What? Don't you like your drink? Is there something else I can get for you?"

"No, the drinks are great. But next time, can you send the Mercedes?"

"Sure! Wait till you see the Ferrari. It's a prototype of the new eight-cylinder Four-Fifty-Eight Spider. The owner wanted a working model of his real car. That baby's almost hotter than the bartender." Greg laughed.

"We'll be here all afternoon, and maybe all evening." Greg removed the lid and sipped his drink.

***

Sandy sat up and stretched. The ocean had crept closer and the gray clouds billowed above them. The breeze had stiffened and her face itched. She could taste sand. Few people now dotted the beach and her stomach growled for food.

Greg snored next to her. He looked more content than she'd seen him in a long time, and with the three drink lids lined up at his side, one from each of the cars. She suspected he would sleep awhile longer. Sandy covered his pink legs with her beach towel. Good thing he'd left on his T-shirt.

The whirring noise sounded again and the Mercedes approached two men to their right. After they ordered their drinks, the men scanned the beach. They smiled at her. She waved in return.

Contemplating a bathroom run, her stomach snarled again.

The Mercedes revved its little electric engine and sprayed the men with sand as it sped away, but it headed away from LA Car and toward the surf shop next door. Surprised, Sandy waited, but the car didn't reappear. Did it break? What about those men's drinks?

She stood, wiped off the sand, and slipped on her cover-up.

I'll just mosey over to the surf shop and check out the T-shirts. If it gets any chillier, we'll have to buy fleece windbreakers.

Sandy's eyes swept the store, empty of shoppers. Rows of cheap colorful T-shirts, bathing suits, muscle shirts, fleece jackets, and sweatshirts lined the middle. Hats, footwear, and snorkel gear were shelved along the walls, and water-rental items were stacked in the back. The counter stood to the right, filled with sundry sweets, chips, nuts, and gum, but no one was manning the register. The smell of rubber from the masks and flippers permeated the shop, and the Eagles' "Smuggler's Blues" played over the sound system.

She listened, but couldn't detect the whirring sound from the car, only muffled voices in a back room. Sandy edged toward the sounds, picking up flip-flops, hats, and snorkels to look like a customer. She found the Mercedes resting on the floor outside the back-room office.

"Winston will be at LA Car, showing off that new six-hundred-sixty-horsepower SRT Viper. Probably got it free. Not a bad perk for being a fuckin' bigwig at Viper headquarters. What an asshole. Since he bought LA Car and this shop, he's been even harder to deal with. Making me a manager as a cover, what kind of bullshit is that? He better bring me what I need this time, that's all I have to say. Then I'm outta here. I have to deliver soon!"

Could he be talking about swimwear? Maybe it's drugs!

"Si, Eddie," a man with the Spanish accent agreed. "Un pequeño problema."

"Maybe, Juan, but maybe not."

A hand touched Sandy's shoulder and she jumped.

"I didn't mean to scare you."

Sandy twisted around and came face to face with a blonde, teenage girl in one of the cheap T-shirts and short-shorts.

"Oh! You didn't, really. I was just ... in a different world." Sandy forced a smile, the frantic beats of her heart starting to slow.

"Can I help you find something?" the teenager asked.

"Well, I was just, uh, fantasizing about learning to dive. Can you show me the scuba equipment?" Sandy walked up to the tanks next to LA Car's Mercedes. "Do you teach scuba diving?"

At that moment, a heavy, tan-skinned, middle-aged man emerged. He stood about her height, with dark hair and light eyes, and a very thick mustache. He picked up the car, slipped an envelope inside the glove compartment, closed the compartment and the door, and placed the car on the floor. "Home," he said.

That must be Eddie, Sandy thought, as the Mercedes revved to life with a high-pitched squeal.

It sped by her and over the teenager's foot, then headed out the door.

"Ow! Shit!" the teenager screamed.

"You okay?" Sandy asked.

"Yeah. That happens a lot."

"It does? So the cars come to the surf shop a lot? Sandy asked.

"Yeah, we get food and drinks from them."

That tall man must realize the bartender can hear and see him through the car, right?

Sandy glanced inside the back door and saw a man with completely salt-and-pepper hair and black eyes. Deep lines in uneven patterns creased his leather-like skin. That must be Juan, she thought.

"I'm Nikki. Did you want to take scuba lessons? We have a great deal on getting certified."

"Maybe. Why don't you give me all the info and I'll check with my husband?"

"Great. Follow me to the front."

Sandy trailed Nikki and pretended to listen to her short rap on how to get certified for ocean diving.

Did the car go back to the men on the beach or to the restaurant?

As soon as she could, Sandy thanked the girl, scooted out of the shop, and spotted Greg reading *Car* magazine with the towel over his crossed legs.

No Mercedes in view. The two men were sipping what appeared to be fruity drinks with slices of orange on the rims. Then she saw the Mercedes driving over the patio and through the doors of the restaurant.

So another car must have brought them their drinks. Hmm ... the bartender. He did hear everything.

What would Greg do if this was his case? He'd probably try to find this Winston character, the asshole.

Greg spotted her and waved. She returned the wave, and then turned to spy on the back of LA Car, open to Hollister Avenue off Bernard Way. Winston hadn't shown yet, at least not in his new Viper. If she could coax Greg into an early dinner at LA Car restaurant, she might be able to learn more about the suits, the cars, the surf shop, the bartender, and what that guy, Eddie, was waiting for. What if the cars doubled as delivery vehicles for contraband or laundered cash? Drugs? What if the restaurant and shop were fronts for crime syndicates? How exciting!

She had no proof, only suspicions that illegal drugs were being dispensed through the remote-control cars. The suited men were probably in on it, too.

Sandy walked up and eased down next to Greg, who flung the magazine into the beach bag. "Where did you go? I woke up and you were gone." Greg pecked her on the cheek.

"Thought I'd check out the surf shop for fleece jackets. It's getting chilly, and I'm hungry."

A real 660 Viper drove around LA Car's driveway. "Wow!" Greg exclaimed. "Let's go check that out—on our way in to eat."

Greg stood, folded the blanket, and dropped it, the lotion, and the water into the bag. He wiped the sand from his legs, slipped into his flip-flops, and flung the beach bag over his shoulder.

As they approached the Viper, a tall handsome man headed into the restaurant. Blond, and in an expensive suit, he looked like a congressman.

Sandy peeked in at the front and back seats, searching for any papers or clues.

"What are you looking at?" Greg asked.

"Oh, the interior. It looks so lush, doesn't it?"

"Yep," Greg said as he circled the car. "The whole car is luscious."

From a distance, sirens could be heard. Greg and Sandy ignored them until they screeched behind them. They turned toward the noise. A police car stopped at the surf shop followed by an ambulance.

"Jeez! I was just in there," Sandy said, watching paramedics jump out and rush into the shop. "I wonder what happened? Want to go and see?"

"No. I told you, I'm not getting involved in any police activities." Greg returned his gaze to the Viper. He backed up to study the lines of the car. "Beautiful, just beautiful. I was hoping Viper would come out with a faster, sportier model, and it did. I read somewhere that they just changed the design again and the next version will be even more luscious, and quicker."

I got to get back to that shop!

"Greg, I'm going over to the shop and check it out. It could be Nikki, the teenager I just talked to. I'll be right back."

"Huh? We're on vacation. You *check out* emergencies everyday. Give it a rest."

"I have to go. I won't be long."

"I'll go in and get us a table." Greg frowned.

Inside the shop's door, near the register, Nikki held her hands over her mouth. Tears streamed down her cheeks. "Oh, my God! Oh, my God!"

"What happened?" Sandy asked.

Nikki removed her hands from her face. "One minute, Eddie was sipping from a drink. The next, he was breathing weird, his face turned bright red, then blue, then purple. Then he grabbed for the shelf like he was dizzy, missed, and keeled over! He was wheezing, and then he stopped." She gasped, "He choked to death! It was horrible! I didn't know what to do. I don't know the Heimlich move, or is it movement. Should I have tried to save him?"

A drink? A drink from LA Car?

"How do you know that he's dead?"

"The paramedics said he was dead!" She sniffled. "Eddie was so nice. I really liked him. A great manager." She bowed her head into her hands and wept. "I did like him and I didn't do anything to save him."

"I'm so sorry." Sandy rubbed her shoulders.

"Hey." Greg appeared at the door and eyed the place. "Looks like everything is under control here. Our table is ready. Let's go." He nodded to Nikki.

Sandy touched Nikki's shoulder. "I'm so sorry, but I have to go," she said and left with Greg.

"Wait until you see the place! Pictures of cars everywhere. The booths are car seats, and the salt and pepper shakers are old cigarette lighters! They have part of a piston as a sugar holder! Wonderful! Let's eat and enjoy this place. Hell, I'm starved. Everything looks under control next door. Let's just enjoy the dinner, Okay?"

"Okay. I'm starved, too."

Sandy mulled over her options as they headed for the restaurant. Maybe she should tell the police about the envelope, and what Juan and Eddie spoke about.

Do I really want to get involved, especially after yelling at Greg about his work?

Yes.

Eat first.

What information did Eddie think he would be getting, a drug bust, a drug deal? Maybe he was a dealer? What did a real dealer look like?

She didn't realize that she was charging toward the restaurant like a soldier on a mission.

"Hey, slow down!"

"Oh, sorry. Just thinking about, well, Nikki seeing all that," she lied.

***

Sandy almost gasped aloud. Juan was talking to Winston and the two suited men behind the reservation desk. The desk resembled an old Buick dashboard with instrument panel, driving wheel, and radio facing them.

"It's from a 1965 Buick Skylark," Greg said. "Isn't it incredible?"

"Yes, incredible!" Sandy studied the dashboard.

Winston stopped whispering to the others and approached. "Where do you want to sit?" Winston asked, acting as a receptionist.

"The bar." Sandy wanted to start there. The all-seeing bartender knew something.

"The bar?" Greg asked, eyes wide. "You *hate* sitting at bars."

"Go right in," Winston waved them in.

"Did you hear what happened at the surf shop?" Sandy

blurted out. "We just saw them take out a body. Scary. Someone said it was one of the owners," she lied again. "Did you know him?"

"Not well," Winston responded coolly.

"Did you?" Sandy asked Juan.

"We deliver drinks, mostly sodas, to the people at the shop. In return, they don't carry any drinks. Customers and the employees have to come here or use our little cars."

"That seems like a good arrangement," Sandy responded, aware that Juan had evaded the question. "Oh, those remote-control cars are so imaginative. Who takes care of them when they break down?"

Juan scowled. "I do. Why?"

"They work so hard. Did you know that the tires spray sand on people?"

The old man shrugged. Winston grinned.

"Let's go." Greg nudged her toward the bar. "You're a regular magpie."

The bar faced the ocean. The brown granite counter sat twelve people and three seats were available.

"What's going on, Sandy?" Greg raised a brow. "You sound like Colombo/Sherlock Holmes/Inspector Poirot."

"Nothing, Greg. I was just curious, that's all. You're hung up on your cars and I was just watching what was happening around us."

He smiled. "Right. That's usually my job. Let's talk more about your job, and your brother, and your mother, and how they are *really* doing."

"I don't want to talk about them. Aren't we here to get away from all of that?"

"Good. Then let's talk about us." Greg placed his hand on her shoulder, drew her into him, kissed her cheek, and rubbed her arm. "I love you."

"Can I help you lovebirds?" a tall bald bartender, with broad shoulders and a nipped waist, asked.

"Honey?" Greg pointed to Sandy.

"Margarita with salt." Sandy studied the bartender and the area near him. "Where do the cars come into the bar?"

"I'll have the same," Greg ordered. "And that's a good question. Where do the cars come in?"

"Right behind the other side of the bar, where the guy with the white hair is."

They both glanced at Juan at the other end of the bar, but Winston was gone.

Sandy stood, "I'm going to the ladies' room. I'll be right back."

"Okay," Greg said.

"Order me a burger with cheddar, no fries unless they have sweet potato."

She would have to work fast.

First, see if the Viper is there, then zip over to the shop and see if Nikki's still there. Maybe the police are questioning her.

Sandy raced out the back. The Viper was gone. Winston left? She jogged to the back of the surf shop near the parking lots. Greg was facing the other way at the bar, but one couldn't be too cautious with a PI husband.

A police car pulled out of the surf shop driveway and onto Hollister. She stepped through the back door of the shop and saw Nikki, her purse over her shoulder and a large set of keys in her hand. Red blotches covered her swollen face.

"Are you okay?" Sandy asked, startling the teenager.

"Oh, it's you." Nikki placed a key in the door and spread both hands out in front of her. "What a horrible afternoon. They asked so many questions. I'm tired. I'm gonna go home, have a joint and some Scotch, listen to music, call my friends, and forget this day ever happened."

"Oh, well, that's understandable," Sandy consoled her.

California girls, I guess.

"I know it must be so upsetting," Sandy said.

Sandy heard a car drive up, a loud sports car. A car door opened.

"Yeah, the manager choked to death. Horrible." Nikki looked over Sandy's shoulder. "Oh, hi, Mr. Parnell. Terrible day today."

Sandy turned and stood face to face with Mr. Parnell, Mr. Winston Parnell.

"Yes, and you did very well, Nikki. Thank you so much for talking to the police, and for all you've done."

"Oh, thank you, Mr. Parnell." Nikki nodded. "I still can't believe all this happened!" Tears welled up in her eyes.

"I know. Neither can I. Go home and rest."

"Thanks." Nikki half-waved to Sandy as she passed.

Winston edged into Sandy's personal space. "Well, well. You seem to be very interested in what happened here."

Like a cauldron of acid, her stomach burned. "I thought, I mean, I thought you said you didn't really know the guy, I mean the owner."

"You need to leave." Sweeping his hand toward the door, Winston almost hit Greg, who was sticking his head around the corner.

"There you are. You okay, Sandy?"

"Yes. I was just leaving. Nikki is fine."

Greg followed her out.

"I was just asking Nikki, who works here, how she was

doing, and he showed up." Sandy exhaled a loud breath. "He knew the guy that was killed."

"Killed? What are you talking about? How in the world do you know that what happened here was murder? What's going on, Sandy? Is this to teach me a lesson? To show me what it looks like from your side of the marriage? Are you trying to investigate a man's death?"

"Nope. Just wondering how Nikki was. I like her, Greg. Now let's eat."

"I don't believe you," Greg said. "In fact, this whole thing is pissing me off."

"How does it feel, Greg? Anyway, you don't have to believe me. You have more of a suspicious mind than I do."

***

Greg paid for the burgers then suggested a walk on the beach. A yellow glow emerged from under the fortress of pearl-gray clouds and dappled the ocean with dancing light. Sandy grabbed Greg's hand and decided to drop the surf-shop mystery. They kicked off their flip-flops and let the cool, hard sand move through their toes.

"That glow is lovely, isn't it?" Sandy said, "I really love the ocean."

"Yeah."

A cool breeze chilled Sandy, still wearing the bathing-suit cover-up. "Are you ready to go back, honey? I'm getting chilly."

They ambled toward LA Car Restaurant on the way home. The Viper was parked outside again, and the three suited men stood near the car talking.

"Well, there's Mr. Winston Parnell with the two men I saw walking into the restaurant this morning."

Sandy watched Greg glanced around the restaurant.

"It's a different culture here than we're used to back home." Then he asked, "Were you bored today? I drank three margaritas too fast, and you only had one. Then I fell asleep. I'm sorry."

"Oh no! You were fine. I had fun watching everything going on at the beach. I'm usually the one reading magazines and drinking, then snoozing, while you spy on the people."

They neared the road behind the car and men. Sandy examined the situation.

"How do you think things would get passed around, like illegal things? Do you think they might hire valets to do that? Wouldn't valets be in a position to pass info, or whatever, between people, like a middleman for drug deliveries?"

"You're killing me. You don't want me to get involved in anything here, just relax, but you're up to your eyeballs in some imaginary case, some whimsical mystery. I thought you didn't like hearing about my work anymore?"

"Actually, many of your stories are intriguing," Sandy said. "Feel free to continue sharing them with me, honey. Really, I do enjoy them, just not the deception."

"That's changing, Sandy. But listen, nothing's going on here. Trust me. The man choked on an olive. The cars were delivering drinks."

Sandy stopped and faced Greg. She believed Eddie was murdered. Nikki's description of his death didn't fit the reaction to choking. She'd seen choking victims. They stayed put while they gasped for air, and grabbed their throats. Eddie didn't.

But what should she tell Greg?

Greg locked on to her eyes. "Come back to me, honey. You're drifting off."

"Oh, yeah. I was thinking you're right. Wanna have a drink before we go home?"

"Sure," Greg said and angled toward the restaurant. "No more murders to solve, okay?"

"Okay." She kissed his lips. "I love you."

"I knew it." He placed his arms on her thin shoulders, and kissed her lips, then nose, then cheek, then forehead.

She giggled.

"I love you so much." Greg kissed her lips again.

They put on their flip-flops and meandered toward the back entrance of the restaurant near the cars. Greg held her hand. "It was weird realizing you were up to something and not knowing what it was." He looked down at the sand as they walked. "Made me nutsy. Helpless."

"See?"

"Yes, I do."

As they entered the restaurant, the noise level assaulted them. Happy Hour had taken over the bar. Loud music replaced the soft sounds of the evening tide, and deafening voices replaced their murmurs of love.

"Let's go home!" Greg yelled.

"I gotta pee, then we'll go!" Sandy pointed to the ladies' room.

"Don't get lost! I'll wait out back near the car! Too loud in here!"

Sandy headed into the bar's ladies' room. There was a line. She'd go to the one in the dining room, she thought, but checked outside for Greg.

She went out the front entrance toward the Viper. The car and the men were gone, and no sign of Greg. Odd, she thought. Maybe Greg went to the men's room. She walked off the parking area and over a few small bushes onto the sand, then headed toward the patio and the ocean view dining room.

She heard whispering. She stopped short, removed her flip-flops, and edged closer to the voice; it was coming from behind a tree not far from her. The clouds muted the stars, and the white-crested ocean smacked against the sand.

"Si, no Eddie. Los tengo. Si, they're folded," Juan whispered.

Folded?

Her heart beat faster. *Can you fold drugs,* she wondered?

"Parnell quiere dos millones," Juan responded.

Two million? That's a lot of drugs. Maybe folded drugs cost more. Boy, California's weird.

"Si, peanuts." Juan seemed to be the only one there.

Peanuts? Two mil is peanuts to the drug lords?

"Si, Nikki did bueno," Juan continued.

She inhaled a short breath.

Peanuts! It was an allergic reaction! To peanuts! Juan killed Eddie!

"Tomorrow, Ferrari."

Folded drugs to Ferrari. Boy, the rich can afford anything.

"Si, hasta mañana."

Shit!

Sandy turned to run, and bounced into Nikki standing behind her.

Nikki pushed Sandy to the sand. "She was listening, Juan. She heard it all," Nikki said in a loud whisper. She stood over Sandy, who lifted herself off the sand to her knees, balanced her body, then stood.

Juan shook his head.

"I was just walking to the patio doors." Sandy pointed

toward the dining room, enveloped in darkness. "There's a line for the bathroom in the bar."

"What are we going to do?" Nikki asked.

"No es bueno," Juan hissed. Then he studied Sandy and shook his head.

Sandy turned to Nikki. "I thought you liked Eddie. You were crying."

"Acting lessons. I'm an actor." Nikki shrugged. "I liked him, a little."

Greg stepped from behind the tree. He held a small flashlight that illuminated the situation. "Hey, Sandy. What are you doing here?"

"Huh?" Sandy stared at him as if in a dream.

Juan placed his hand in his pocket and withdrew a small gun.

"I don't think so, Mr. Velasquez," a police officer said, gun drawn, as he stepped into view.

Sandy stared at the gun in the policeman's hand.

Nikki gasped.

Oh my God!

White stars flashed in front of Sandy's eyes. Her world went black.

***

Did I die? Is heaven really all white?

Sandy fluttered her eyelids to adjust to the white light. Where *am I?*

"Hey, love. How ya feeling?"

Sandy focused in on Greg's concerned face. "What happened?"

"You fainted."

"I'm so sorry, honey. Jesus, I don't know what I was thinking!" Sandy rubbed her temples and felt the condo's white leather couch under her. She stared into Greg's eyes. "I had no idea how dangerous your job was! I thought you just sat in your car for hours spying on cheating husbands and wives."

"Well, mostly," Greg said as he sat beside her and pulled her into his arms. "You did well for your first case. Most of what you suspected was accurate." He kissed the hair on the side of her head.

"Yeah?" Sandy pulled back, sniffled, and edged up on the couch, leaving room for Greg to sit next to her. Her ankle throbbed. She glanced at the white rug, white furniture, white TV, and grabbed a white tissue from the end table for her nose.

"Yessiree. Winston Parnell was selling Viper company secrets and car designs for millions to Eddie, a middleman to a new car company. Juan worked for Parnell and double-crossed Eddie. Thanks to you, the police discovered it was the LA Car's gimmick cars that exchanged the plans and the money. The bartender was in on it, too."

"When did you know?"

"When I saw one of the items that Eddie knocked over when he reached for the shelf."

Sandy visualized the scene. "The peanuts, right?"

"I remembered when that seven-year-old boy died of a severe anaphylactic shock to peanuts in your hospital." He smiled. "That's when I went to the police."

Sandy rubbed her temples. "I never thought that Juan guy would pull out a gun!"

"Last-ditch effort from a murderer." Greg shook his head. "What were they going to do with our bodies? Just leave them for someone to stumble over?"

Sandy giggled. "Could you see them trying to pull my body in the sand past the patio with the patrons at the windows trying to eat? Then pull your body along the same path to the ocean? Imagine the faces?"

Greg laughed.

Sandy exhaled. "Well, tomorrow I'm staying in the condo, reading my magazines, and occasionally staring out at the ocean. That's it. The end."

Psychic Spies

A gust of wind snatched yellow and red leaves from a massive old oak that towered over a peeling, white, converted barracks, number 2460, at Fort George G. Meade, Maryland.

Tommy Dawson tried to catch a bright red leaf as it swirled near him, but he missed and it fell onto the sidewalk. He headed into the offices for Stargate. All the doors were unmarked, completely devoid of any signs or words identifying what went on behind them. The US Army wasn't anxious to reveal a project that employed paranormal activity. But today, in October of 1979, both China and Russia were years ahead of the US in the military application of psychic abilities. They had already found US installations and were scanning secret codes.

Tommy was a remote viewer. He used extrasensory perception to obtain information about practically anything, from McDonald's to missiles, separated from him by time, distance, or obstacles. He didn't have the multifaceted abilities of Zan, but he'd just made it to the big time by remote viewing not only a Russian missile-base location, but a secret command post fifty miles from the base. Both targets were pinpointed, and that information was shared with select intelligence agencies. Covert operatives in Russian would utilize the information to identify, and in some cases assassinate, important Soviets. It was a small but vital contribution to US victory in the Cold War.

The aroma of fresh coffee greeted him inside 2460, along with his younger brother John Dawson, nicknamed "Radar" because of his superior telepathic receiver abilities, as well as his talent for detecting the general area of the sender. Radar stood holding a coffee mug in front of a bare, antique, oak office desk that dominated a corner of the room.

Tommy and Radar hardly resembled each other. Radar's shiny chestnut hair was chopped at his shoulders, and round, wire-rim, John Lennon glasses framed his dark-chocolate eyes. He stood a head shorter, and was much thinner, than Tommy. He wore a tight, gray, button-down shirt tucked into his black slacks, outlining muscles Tommy envied. Tommy had the height, the weight, the brown beard and mustache, and the ice blue eyes that his disco queens loved, along with his dimples.

Tommy and Radar were the only two civilians at the office, and both were chosen, from about a hundred men and after several days of testing, for their special gifts. Even though they were a year apart, they had extrasensory perception like their mom. Now, they both were drowning in a sea of eggheads and army brass.

Today, though, Radar seemed heavy. Something was weighing him down.

Tommy slipped off his tan leather jacket and threw it on the backless, worn-out green couch opposite the desk.

He rubbed his arms, covered by a V-neck mahogany velour sweater with a white stripe running down each arm. "Frigid, man. Colder than a witch's you-know-what in here."

"Yeah," Radar answered from somewhere far away. After a long pause, he added, "I just turned on the heat."

"How's it hangin'?" Tommy asked as he poured coffee into a Styrofoam cup from the Mr. Coffee machine on a metal stand next to the desk.

"He's after me, man. He's hunting me. It's a dude. I can feel him." Radar's shoulders dropped as he headed into the large conference room. "I don't know how he's doing it, man, but he's doing it to me."

Tommy, concerned, followed him in, foregoing the cream for his coffee. He gazed at the oversized golden-framed photo of President Carter, next to another over-sized golden-framed photo-collage of a collage of the other presidents, hanging on the long wall opposite the door. Both made him feel solemn, and important, and watched; his concern for the hostages was also reignited. A black-board on wheels stood to the right of the presidents, with different-colored chalk resting on a wooden ledge.

Radar plopped into one of the swivel armchairs and exhaled. "No doubt about it. The dude's after me." He placed his coffee mug on the long conference table.

Tommy eased into the armchair next to him and pushed the chair back with his feet to accommodate his long legs. "Who's after you? What dude? Does it have to do with one of the tests?" He stroked his beard with both hands, then rubbed his mustache as if pasting it down on his lip.

"I don't know. That's what's freaking me out. It's like

he can get under my skin, Tommy, you know? He's got my frequency now, man. I'm telling you."

Tommy touched Radar's left shoulder. "When did you first sense him?"

"Day before yesterday. Day I picked up the Trans Am."

"Tell me about the telepath," Tommy asked, thinking about the high-performance car Radar drooled over since they'd seen the movie *Smokey and the Bandit*. He drooled over women, the taller the better, with limber bodies and soft skin who could dance like the Sex-O-Lettes in *Saturday Night Fever*.

"It happened just like it did to Kamensky with Monin and Nikolaiev. You remember reading about Kamensky? Fifty-nine? Sixty? I read all about them. This came from out of nowhere, man. I was cruising on Route 32, heading for 95, and like boom! Instant headache, a brain drain like I never felt ... then there he was, in my head. I couldn't make him out. He was like in a dark fog. I couldn't breathe, man, couldn't breathe! Like he was trying to suffocate me, man!"

Since joining Stargate, Tommy had heard some far-out shit about telepathy, but suffocating someone?

Radar stood to pace behind his chair. "He sent pulses, like loads of them at a time. Hit me like a sledgehammer, right in the chest. I started to hyperventilate. It was all I could do to get home and into the apartment. I took a cold shower and it got better. At first I thought I would faint, but I didn't. Suddenly, everything seemed totally negative, like the whole world had gone wrong around me. It was just like Kamensky wrote about, the hyper-synchronized waves. My body started to shake and my head ached, like the worst migraine. I didn't know what to do."

"What *did* you do?"

"After the cold shower, I smoked some weed." Radar stopped and glared at Tommy, hands splayed in defeat.

"How long did the drain last?"

"I don't know. The weed blocked him." Radar plopped back down and sipped his coffee. "Well, that and 'I Will Survive.' I kept singing, and I got hoarse. Man, my throat ached."

Tommy laughed. The last thing he'd expected was Donna Summer.

"It worked. I sang and sang and sang that song till he could feel I was out to get him, too. Then, I crashed, man. Conked out like the grateful dead."

Tommy studied his brother.

"You gotta help me. We have to find him. I know he's in Moscow, but that's it."

"Is he Russian?"

"Yeah, Russian. Definitely Russian. Should we tell the Major?"

"Good question. I don't know yet. Can you send messages yet? You said that you were working on it."

"Actually, this was the first time that it felt like I'd sent something. Donna Summer, man! I think it got through to him."

Tommy laughed again. Disco, he thought, could win the Cold War.

"This isn't funny! I'm too open. Everything walks right in and sits right down, man. It doesn't even have to knock. It's like I have a huge portal, and it pours right through. This last time was the worst. I don't even know where the idea to sing came from. But I kept singing and singing. Any louder and he would've heard me through his ears. Maybe I should have sung something else ... 'Taps' or something."

"Nah, you were right on. Keep singing if he comes back. We'll find him."

Radar relaxed, then tensed up again. "I think he wants me dead. Why? And why now?" He glanced at his watch. "Ten-ten in the morning here, ten-ten at night there. Thank God there's a time difference. I get breathing room when he sleeps. I can feel free to dream for me."

Tommy's antennae vibrated and red-warning waves shimmered behind his eyes. Zan, his mentor and 2460's best paranormal agent, should be on this, he thought. What if the telepathic sender worked with a viewer and the Russians made their location? Tommy stood. "I'll be right back."

"Where are you going?" Radar sounded nervous. "Maybe you shouldn't leave."

"Chill man, going to get Zan. I want to do a viewing. He can monitor."

"I thought you didn't need a monitor anymore?"

"Better to have Zan, so I can keep all my senses open and directed. Go wait in the RV room." Tommy pointed to the next room. "I'll be there in a minute." He ran to fetch Zan. He needed Zan to help him with his brother. Zan would be more objective.

***

Tommy and Zan walked into the remote viewing room. Zan and Tommy looked eerily alike. Zan was tall and chunky, with a beard and mustache, and thick black hair and black eyes. He sat down at the head of the short, narrow table in the center of the remote viewing room. Tommy sat opposite him, paper and pencil in hand. Mind on the task at hand.

A large tape recorder sat on the table. A TV camera,

for session documenting or viewing from another room, was mounted on the wall. The room was painted a neutral eggshell color, with acoustic tiles on the walls and lights set low by dimmers to minimize distractions.

Tommy picked up the unlined white sheets of paper and tapped them on the table to even the edges, then set the pile down in front of him, a signal to calm his thoughts and body.

"Let's get to work," Zan said tersely. "Radar, leave and go into the next room, so you don't interfere in any way. Write down anything you receive. We'll compare notes after the session. I'll start the recording when I give you the first clue, Tommy."

"You should do the viewing," Radar said to Zan.

"Tommy can do it. You concentrate on messages coming in and write them down. That's your expertise. Use it. We won't let anything happen to you. You'll be okay. Now, just do your job."

Radar left, shoulders slumped.

Tommy closed his eyes. He would need two to three minutes to center himself, calm his mind, and block out the room.

Tommy had graduated the remote viewing program, all six stages: following an imagined signal line to the remote site; studying the site with sensory values; viewing the site's structures in 2D, usually buildings, but also bridges, airfields, and two days ago, the silo; then broadening the scope by searching out sites for which he could discern technical areas, such as the one he was sitting in right now; then detecting tracking centers, like radar, sonar, and satellite; then, lastly, adding the third dimension to the site, to identify size and importance.

Tommy was like their mother; he'd always been able

to sense what people were feeling. To do so remotely was an ability he could never have imagined. If he could get the skinny on Radar's Russian dude, he'd be ranked up there with McMoneagle, who'd predicted, last April, that Richard Queen, one of the Iran hostages, would get sick with MS symptoms and be sent home. Queen was sent home in July. That gave the project some wings.

"Concentrate," Zan whispered. "You are not concentrating."

Tommy nodded.

"Moscow," Zan prompted.

He didn't have to be coaxed any further through the stages. He tapped into his signal line and attuned himself to it, and through it proceeded to exploring major structures of the site—like the strongest telescope, he zoomed into Moscow, focusing on a general area, then zooming in further. He examined the shapes and forms, hard and soft, domed or angular, and their colors, for example, the deep green glow of nuclear material he sometimes glimpsed. He also received impressions via his other senses: a smell of sulfur, oil, or fried potatoes, the sound of a jet engine in the distance, the feel of a stiff cold breeze on his skin. Then he tuned into the emotional atmosphere. Was there fear and pain, like in some of the prisons, torture chambers, and drug-testing sites? Or was there kindness and love being given to animals and people in some of the service buildings he scanned?

His visual aperture opened and his signal line widened. Beyond thought, his hand moved. He drew on the plain paper as he crossed over invisible lines to the last stage. There was a steeple, a cross, a church. A human form. Tommy shaded in his shape and roughed out his facial features, then placed an arrow next to him, pointing upward.

Lines protruded from the form's middle like a bursting star. A big man? A big building. But it had energy. It was a life-form.

He'd found him. It was Radar's dude. He didn't know how he knew. He just knew.

Tommy spoke. "A tall dark man. Angry. Standing, looking ... holding something. Studying something outside."

"Look around you," Zan prompted. "What else do you see?"

"A church-like structure. He's next to it, in some kind of enclosure, with an opening, a ... window?"

He had to be careful not to allow his mind's natural tendency, identifying and labeling, to touch the extrasensory signal line. That would produce an analytical overlay, and he'd have to break the line. The conscious thinking mind was the ultimate distraction; in trying to determine whether the opening was a door, or a window, or even a crumbled wall, the ESP, from his subconscious, would no longer be working, and the session would be lost.

"He's in his home. Does he have pictures on the walls?" Zan moved the session along.

Tommy scanned the walls. The viewing was resolving, coming into focus. Several prints of still-life paintings hung next to family photographs.

"Keep looking around. Don't stop. Do you smell anything?"

"Stew, I think."

"Can you tell what he is holding?"

Tommy was also starting to feel as though he was being watched, like on a camera—even though no one in Russia could possibly see him. Was Radar's Russian dude opening himself up as a receiver, so a remote viewer on his end might play back at them? He slowed his breathing and started to draw. Thin veils of plasma started to form in front of him, making viewing more difficult. A sketch? Was he holding a sketch, a drawing, a painting? No, not a painting.

"He's holding a sketch?" Zan asked, studying the drawing. "Of what?"

"It's a man .... with shoulder-length hair, round wire-rim glasses ... Oh, my God! It's Radar! He's holding a picture of Radar!"

Suddenly, Radar started singing "I Will Survive" from the other room.

As Radar's voice grew louder, presumably blocking the Russian, Tommy felt more watched, invaded, and breathless. Man, this whole thing was getting too weird and intense. Luckily, unlike Radar, he could disconnect from the signal line—without having to disturb the greater atmosphere with off-key clamor. Poor Radar, he thought. So much harder was his work.

Tommy could sense Zan leave the room. He shut down the session, then needed a few minutes to refocus and return to the reality of ... Ft. Meade. He rubbed his eyes and scratched his ears. Oh man, poor Radar, Tommy thought. What a drag to be so open! How tired and depressed he must be.

His thoughts turned back to the Soviet he'd viewed. He was dark-skinned, African? Egyptian? Or just a swarthy Russian? Was he a remote viewer or a telepathic sender, or just a scientist? How did he get a sketch of his brother? Damn it!

Gripping the pencil, Tommy drew as much of the possible Russian agent as he could remember before the image faded. With any luck, Major Thomas Hunter, the commander of the project and a firm believer in ESP, could identify the man by comparing Tommy's sketch to his files of known Soviet operatives.

Muffled voices came from the next room. Radar grew more volatile and his voice rose louder and higher as the conversation continued. Tommy tried, but failed, to discern the words. Remote viewing always exhausted him. He could barely think, no less hear the happenings in the next room.

Suddenly, there was silence in both rooms.

Tommy waited a few seconds before stepping back into the conference room.

Radar seemed in a trance, totally out to lunch, and Zan held up his hand like a traffic cop. Tommy halted under the doorjamb.

They stood, motionless, for several minutes, until Radar's shoulders relaxed and he turned his head toward Tommy with a glare straight out of *The Exorcist*.

"He's singing your song, Tommy," Radar said. "See me ... feel me ... touch me ... heal me..." Radar smirked. "He's after you, too, brother." He turned toward Zan. His eyes fluttered, his face turned white, his eyes rolled backward, and he fell off his chair and onto the floor.

"I'll get help. You stay with him." Zan bolted out the door without checking Radar.

Tommy knelt next to Radar and groped for his pulse. It felt like little beads of pearls flowing slowly under Tommy's fingers. He squeezed Radar's hand. "You hang in there. You got a new Bandit to ride. We'll get through this together. Don't you leave me here all alone with the Army and the eggheads. Think Donna Summer. Sing her song in your head. I will survive. We will survive this, together."

***

"I can't go home, man!" Radar had yelled when Tommy picked him up at the army infirmary later that day. "What am I going to do, sit there and watch *Hart to Hart? Trapper John, MD?* I can't go to bars like you do. I'd have to stay stoned. I feel crazy, Bro. Really crazy!"

"Okay, I'll drive you to Bandit and you can follow me home."

"Oh no. Huh-uh. I'm not driving!"

"Why the hell not?"

"You saw him! The dude was holding my picture! He's holding it, man, and his abilities are more powerful than mine! He could kill me while I'm driving. Right off the road, off a cliff."

"Yeah?"

"You didn't do any reading, did you?" Radar asked and didn't wait for an answer. "Albert Nichols? 1966? The article about the Soviet, Kotkov, who used telepathy to knock this girl totally out, simply by focusing on strong images of her sleeping?"

"Knocked her out?"

"Yeah, man! Rendered her unconscious. Dropped her on the spot. Flat on her back, from across town."

"You read too much. You're turning into an egghead. Do you feel him anymore?" Tommy asked as they walked up the steps to his two-bedroom apartment.

"No, and he better not find me either. Radar is shut down for repairs. All I want to do is smoke a joint and scarf down chips and dip, the sour-cream-and-onion-soup-mix kind. You have that?"

Tommy smiled as he unlocked his door. "Yep, and

some beer. And I even have healthy food, some popcorn, and hot dogs."

He opened the door and Radar yelled as Tommy's German shepherd, Shep, jumped up in welcome. Radar petted him. "Sorry, boy, didn't expect you to come at me from the side. Y'almost gave me a heart attack. Peace." Shep licked Radar's hand.

***

"Alexander Neviev," Major Hunter had said earlier as he dropped a file in front of Zan and Tommy onto the conference table. "Neviev's wife was killed by one of our agents near the command post. She was a major asset for the Russians. He probably wants revenge. Neviev's a telepathic sender and receiver. He's good. Got a lot of intel on him and his wife."

As he opened the refrigerator for a beer, Tommy's heart pounded in his chest. The threat to Radar pulled him into the hard core reality of this psychic Cold War; how many lives were secretly snuffed, aided by his psychic powers? His abilities had killed people, maybe some of them innocent, but all of them unsuspecting. Today, he felt like his powers were a curse and not a gift.

Maybe it wasn't so cool being a part of all this. Zan, his mentor, had said he would be the one of best remote viewers in another year. Now he wasn't so sure he wanted any of it.

"I'll be home in a couple of hours. I'm going back in, to do another viewing." Tommy handed the beer to Radar. "Don't leave."

"Leave? Where the hell would I go? I'm planted. Beer, dip, Shep, and *The Price is Right*."

"Stay cool." Tommy placed his hand on the doorknob

and opened the front door, then turned to Radar. "Ever feel like you're being watched by a sender? Do they have that type of power?"

"No. I can feel his thoughts inside, nothing outside looking in. You feel like you're being watched?" His voice rose with his eyebrows.

"Not now," Tommy lied, "but during the viewing, while I was in his house. Like I was on *Candid Camera.*"

"This dude is trouble." Radar sat on the couch. "Be careful." Radar snapped his finger and pointed at Tommy. "I read there was another Russian, Victor Milodan, who actually eavesdropped telepathically on a sender and receiver. It's sick, but it happened. It's documented, you know. I wish you had read all the material they gave us, Tommy. This is sick, man, really, really sick. "

"I'm buying you some comics." Tommy grinned and closed the door. Time was of the essence, he thought, as he skipped down the steps to his car, got in, closed the door, and sped away.

Tommy spotted the black Buick Regal tailing him about halfway to the office.

He picked up his military mobile phone, a big black box the base mechanics had installed between the bucket seats. He dialed Major Hunter, then picked up the receiver and held it to his right ear.

"I'm being followed," Tommy said, feeling more nervous than he sounded.

"I'm on Annapolis Road."

"I'll send a car to meet you."

Just as he returned the receiver to the station, the car disappeared. Tommy called back. "They turned off."

"Are you sure you were being followed?"

"I'm not totally sure, but I'm certain of one thing. I'm

being watched. From near or far, I don't know, but since I did the viewing of Neviev's house, I've been feeling eyes on me. Whoever is watching is good, and constant." He surprised himself with the force of his words. His heart pounded again. Sometime in the last day, he'd become the hunted, and a new feeling of compassion touched his heart. The hunted, horrible.

"Go home. Pick up Radar, get some clothes. You're staying at the fort. You'll both be safer here. I'll call Zan and the others. Time for a meeting."

Tommy parked his Bug, got out, and hopped up the sixteen steps to his apartment two at a time. He unlocked the door and rushed into the apartment. The couch was empty, and Shep trotted out of his bedroom. "Radar?" Tommy shouted. His chest hurt and his feet felt like jelly, his foundation weakened as if the floors were made of quicksand.

No answer.

"Radar!"

He darted into his spacious, stark bedroom with clothes strewn on the bed and a corner chair. He scanned the second bedroom, an office with a blown-up mattress on the floor. No Radar.

His telephone rang.

He let it ring until he checked both bathrooms. Did he go for a walk, Tommy wondered? I was only gone about twenty minutes! Where the hell could he go in twenty minutes?

The phone kept ringing and ringing. He answered it.

"Tommy?" A Russian accent.

"Yeah?" Tommy answered, trying to sense something about the person who went with the voice.

"You were in my home in Moscow. You are the reason

my wife was murdered. Now your comrade will soon be dead."

Tommy hung up. He dialed Major Hunter. Breathless, he sputtered, "Neviev! He knows me! He knew my name! He got my phone number! Someone's about to be killed!"

"Well, it's not Radar. He just called. He should be with your downstairs neighbor, Sarah."

"He's not dead?" Tommy sighed.

"He wasn't five minutes ago. Go check. The car is still on the way. Get him and make it quick!" The Major hung up.

Tommy raced down the steps with Shep at his heels. He knocked on Sarah's door. She was a single mom with a three-year-old son, Dalton.

No answer.

He pounded harder. Shep barked.

No answer.

"Shit!"

Suddenly, Shep ran to the end of the building, turned, and disappeared. Tommy loped after him, toward the side yard. Turning the corner, he plowed right into Radar, knocking him over.

"Jesus H. Christ." He helped Radar up. "Are you okay? What happened?"

"He found me again. Got into my head, man. Telling me to go to sleep. I knew it! He's trying to KO me, man! Coldcock me! Lay me out! I didn't want to be alone."

"Sarah?" Tommy looked around.

"She'll be right back. Picking up Dalton from day care."

"Hunter sent a car. Let's go upstairs and get some clothes. Sing a song. I have something to tell you."

Radar started singing "I Want You to Want Me."

Tommy jerked around. "Get real!"

"Sarah. I could dig her. She's dynamite."

"Dream on, Radar. Sing another song."

"Okay. How about, 'MacArthur's Park is melting in the dark, all the sweet green icing flowing down' ..."

"Neviev called."

"What do you mean, he called?"

"On the telephone, man. Damn thing rang, I picked it up, and there he was. He knows me now, too. He knows where I live. And he's not alone. I felt, like, another presence there. More people are involved now."

"Oh man, now I'm scared again." Radar said as he followed Tommy into his bedroom and watched him throw clothes in a backpack.

"Keep singing. No more being scared. He can read your emotions. You told me that. Stop being scared. Get angry! Think of an angry song, not something that's melting."

"Come on, Shep." Tommy threw cans of food into a brown paper bag with his bowl. Let's blow this coop."

"I can't think of an angry song. Sorry." Radar clamped his hands over his ears and squeezed his eyes shut. 'Someone left the cake out in the rain. I don't think that I can take it, 'cause it took so long to ..." He stopped singing, and opened his eyes. "He's gone."

"Good, here comes the car." Tommy opened Sarah's door and let Shep in. He threw the bag on her kitchen floor. "You be good, boy. Keep an eye on Sarah and Dalton. I'll be back."

Tommy stepped out and closed the door. "I'll call Sarah and leave a message on her machine. God, I hope she has it on."

The Lincoln Town Car pulled up to the curb and Tommy and Radar rushed in with their leather gym bags.

Major Hunter sat in the front seat. "Zan's dead," he said flatly.

"What? How?" Radar and Tommy said in unison.

"We don't know. He never responded to the phone call and didn't come in. I sent men over and they found him. A hemorrhage. He had blood coming out of his eyes, ears, and mouth. The Army coroner has taken his body. We won't know how it happened till after the autopsy, if then."

Tommy's stomach turned into a cauldron of acid and his words were whispers. "Neviev said my 'comrade' would soon be dead. I though he meant Radar. I can't believe it was Zan." Tommy shook his head in shock. "He must have all our pictures. But how? Now, we're all exposed. What the hell are we going to do? How can we fight them with Zan gone? *He* has help. I felt more than one person!"

"I called in our best, Tommy. We're having a group remote viewing. Our two top telepaths, both majors you haven't met, are also coming to work with Radar. If anyone can catch those who know about you both, it's them. With luck, they'll also discover who else is on Neviev's list."

***

The group sat around the table with Major Hunter at one head and the two remote viewer majors opposite each other. Ace, tall, thin, and bald, wore his uniform, even though it wasn't mandatory for this project; he sat on Tommy's right. Roger, football-player stocky with thinning brown hair and wire-framed glasses, the expert on finding technology, sat to Tommy's left.

Tommy squirmed. He worried about Radar. Radar and the other two Army-trained telepaths were stationed in the other building, intending to approach the targets from a different direction, which would aid Tommy and the majors to hone in on Neviev's site in Moscow.

Radar would be totally "open" and vulnerable, the hurt sheep exposed to the wolves, but at least he had two other telepaths with him, a sender and receiver. Tommy, meanwhile, would be entering into a battle of the minds. The plan was for the six of them to constitute a psychic attack force that would not only neutralize the Soviet's offensive capabilities, but also overwhelm their defenses. "We'll start in Moscow. First one to find him, write the coordinates down. I'll give the coordinates to the others. We'll go in together."

Everyone nodded.

"When you lock in on your site, look around. Write down everything, so we can follow along with you to determine a location. We need to see where you're going, even if it's a dead end. I have our agents ready in Moscow. They'll move as soon as the exact location is found."

Everyone nodded again.

Tommy didn't know the majors, but he could sense their expertise, seriousness, and commitment. He was happy to have them at his sides, Ace hunting Neviev, and Roger seeking out the technology they were using to infiltrate the Stargate project. Tommy knew exactly what he was looking for: the observer, the one who pulled the strings, the one who, they thought, had Zan killed.

"Moscow. Neviev," Major Hunter said, launching the session as the other connected to their signal lines.

Tommy hooked on his signal line and followed it through the six stages to Neviev's house. But the place felt different. Empty. He wrote "different" and "empty" on a piece of paper, adding "stale air" and "cold." He moved to the bedroom and felt warmth from a big object. He wrote "desk," "warm," "stove."

"Move on, Tommy," Major Hunter's commanded.

Tommy moved through the same opening he had viewed before. He spotted the street, then turned to see the church. "Church," "steeple." The energy of the church drew him toward it. He followed the energy.

Eyes were on him again. One set. He wrote "observer," then pursued the line, with a feeling of descent. Now he was in the church basement. "Dark, "basement," "person," "warm." Tommy moved closer to the energy. "Not Neviev."

"Tommy, good job. Go to a different room," Major Hunter said.

"Ace, good job. Get the exact coordinates. Remember that we need the *exact* coordinates."

"Roger, more words about the computer. Where is it? Draw if you have no words. Be precise."

Tommy now sensed the powerful energy in the church, paranormal energy. The church was at the center of some sort of vortex. Tommy also felt that unseeing eyes were closely monitoring each of his moves. He projected his attention toward the most intense energy. He was surprised when he felt the same pattern present in Neviev's house. Tommy moved toward the shadow. He started to recognize ... No! It couldn't be. Closer and closer he moved. The observer. The paranormal asset who haunted Radar and made him crazy. The observer who made him sing Donna Summer to gain some peace.

"Move to the next room," Hunter ordered.

Tommy stayed. He smelled musk and mold, and the cold was increasing. Then he zeroed in on the observer.

There. Yes. He couldn't believe it, but it was true ... "Zan. It's Zan! He's not dead!"

"Everyone come back. Break your signal lines. That's an order! Our agents are closing in on Neviev and the church. Briefing in ten minutes. "

"I perceived Zan. I really believe it was Zan. But he's dead. Right? But he didn't feel dead. Can that happen? How can that happen?"

"Ten minutes, Tommy." The Major left the room.

Ace stepped up to Tommy with his hand extended. "Good work, son."

Tommy shook his hand. "Thanks. But did we really get Neviev and a paranormal nest?"

The nod of Ace's head described the grim business. They would all be dead soon.

Roger muttered, "In a goddamn church."

***

Tommy was still wondering how the Russians stole their intel when the Major walked back into the room ten minutes later. He glanced at Ace and Roger and said, "Great job, guys. Now, I need to talk to Tommy."

Ace patted Roger's back as they left. "Good job, again. You're one of the finest, boy."

The Major sat down next to Tommy. "We have to talk about Radar."

Tommy thought, Radar? He said, "Not Zan?"

Hunter ignored the question. "Radar is the leak. He didn't do it consciously, but he did do it, and we don't know how much damage he did. We're thinking not too much, and that's good, son. That's very, very good. But I'm not so sure."

"What?! Impossible!"

"What I mean to say is that he's too open. He hasn't mastered control over his skills yet. Advanced telepaths can read him, easily. Zan, at my direction, became the observer. I had him switch to just observing Radar. He did nothing else. We told you both he was dead so Radar wouldn't pick up on him, or think about him."

"Zan's not dead?"

"No." Major Hunter paused.

Tommy waited for him to decide how much to divulge.

"Zan," Hunter hesitated, then said, "Zan went in deeper than anyone's ever been before. He has the skill, the knowledge, and the ability."

"And—"

"And he could find Radar anywhere, at anytime, and read some of his signals and thoughts. Radar compared all the articles he read to what we're doing here, exposing classified information."

"Oh no!"

"They received enough of a signal to get your telephone number. We don't know how they did it or the total extent of the damage."

"What happens now?" Tommy asked, picking up something from Hunter that he didn't want to consider.

"We've just sedated Radar. Zan will try to read him after he's totally under to determine if he's revealing messages while asleep. Unfortunately, Zan thinks that Radar might be hindering the project by totally unintentional means."

Oh, my God! Tommy thought, his antennae vibrating again, and the trusty red warning waves shimmering behind his eyes. He clamped his hands into fists, then forced them to unclench. "What are you going to do?"

"Nothing right now. We need to ascertain the amount

of leaked intel and what collateral damage might occur, and stop it. Of course, Radar will have to ... go dark. Luckily, he wasn't a remote viewer; otherwise, he would have given away every location that is important to us. We have a new drug that will help control his receiving and shut down his minor sending abilities. It's very experimental, but we, uh, believe it will work. It has to work for Radar."

"I'll go visit him. See that he's all right"

"Sure. I understand. He's in good hands, Tommy. Thank you for all your help. You're going to be one of our best assets. You found the Russian command base, the biggest target our project has viewed, and you locked onto Zan too, while he was remote viewing on Radar! You will most certainly go up a pay grade, and when I share all this with the commander, he will want to meet you and make sure you stay on our team. A fine day for America, son. Good job."

"Yes, sir. Thank you, sir. I'll take Radar home with me when he wakes up." Then we're both leaving the project, Tommy thought. We're both flying the coop together. I'll have his Bandit sent home before we leave. But first, I'll need to find us a home. Then I'll remote view Hunter and the others. Make sure they are not planning something bad against Radar. Oh, my God! How the hell did we get into this?

"Sure, son. When he wakes up."

Harry and Penny

Harry Silverstein tapped on the wooden front door of an old, white, split-level house. The sun whispered goodnight behind him and a pre-autumn breeze cooled the back of his neck.

The door swung open and a thin, curly-gray-haired older woman, with big ice-blue eyes, gaped at him. A smile broadened across her wrinkled face.

"Hello, Harry! You're early!" She draped her arms around him and squeezed. She gazed over his shoulder. "Where's the car?"

"Hey, Sis. On the other block, down Redwood," he answered as he glanced at her fuzzy pink slippers, black leotards, and long red sweatshirt embroidered in bold white letters:

If you're lucky enough to fall in love at my age,
use your pharmacy as a bridal registry.

She followed his eyes and chuckled. "It was on sale at

the consignment shop, five bucks on the half-price rack. Got it for two-fifty. One of those red-tag sale days. Who could resist?"

"Love it. Is that grandson of yours here, or are you alone?" Harry asked as he scanned the room behind her.

"Jacob's here, eating me out of house and home, as usual. Wait until you see him! He resembles you more than he does his own dad."

"How's Sophie doing?" he asked as they both stepped into the house and ambled toward the kitchen.

"She's working at the restaurant two nights a week now to buy him all his extras. Tough being a single mom. Her family hasn't contacted her at all since his death. Such sadness. How long can they hold a grudge, over religion, no less." She stared into his eyes. "What's wrong, Harry? It's been months since I've heard from you. Why'd you park the car a block away? Someone following you? You okay?"

"Let's go in. It's getting chilly. I wanna say hello to my grandnephew. We'll talk." He sighed.

"We've worked together for twenty-five years and I know that face. It's one you don't wear often."

"Let's sit." He sat on one of the fifties-style kitchen chairs with a plastic foam pink seat.

He didn't want to think about them possibly being in danger right now. He couldn't shake his gut-level feeling, which he'd had for a while now, that he was being followed, yet he had taken every precaution possible, including borrowing one of his buddies' used cars. Penny's slippers scuffed against the floor as she followed Harry into the kitchen. Harry heard the TV in the next room, and eyed Jacob rushing toward him.

"Hey, Uncle Harry, howzit going?" Jacob passed Harry

and plopped his long lean body into the kitchen chair next to him, devouring half of a peanut butter and jelly sandwich in two bites.

Jacob did, in fact, look like him. Could pass for his son. Jacob was a head shorter though, about five-nine. His curly sandy-blond hair and angular features made him look like a thinner, younger Albert Einstein, but with Penny's ice-blue eyes. Yep, he thought as he studied Jacob. You got my genes.

He winked at Jacob. "You're taller and better looking than last time I was here. The girls must be after you by now." Harry extended his hand. Jacob shook it vigorously and kept shaking while they scrutinized each other.

"Stop with the handshaking, already. You're making me nauseous!" Penny broke their connection. "Harry, you want a beer?"

"Yeah," he said, watching her. "Nice refrigerator." He whistled. "Must have cost a bundle."

"Had to replace the old thing, you know. Motor died. Water all over the place. What a mess. Paid cash." Penny pulled out a beer, twisted off the cap, and handed it to Harry. "You want a sandwich too?"

Harry scanned the contents of the fridge. "Nah. People would give you their food stamps if they saw how little you kept in there."

"Me and my friends still eat out most days. I keep some sandwich meat for the kid."

Harry switched his attention to Jacob. "Tell me what's new. What are you, fifteen?"

Jacob nodded. "Yep, and I'm into baseball." He scanned the kitchen counter. "We got a new coach. He came last week and watched me play. He thinks I'm good. Do you have any chocolate chip cookies, Gram?"

"Hmm, cookies." Penny planted her hands on the table and pushed down to help lift her body. "Yes, I bought the dollar-ninety-nine-cent specials. They give you two long rows of chocolate chip cookies for a dollar-ninety-nine! Of course, you need to have the coupon. God bless Walgreen's. I always have coupons."

Harry watched her pull out the bag of cookies from a faded oak drawer, place it in front of Jacob, split the cover, and pull out the black plastic container.

Jacob grabbed five at once.

"Harry," Penny interjected, "Jacob's new coach thinks he might be a pro someday. Isn't that wonderful? WAH."

"Yeah."

"WAH?" Jacob asked. "What's WAH?"

"Oh, after working so long together, your granduncle and I talk in code sometimes. Keep sentences short. People sometimes think we're nuts. So as I was saying, his coach loves Jacob's eighty-mile-per-hour fastball and slider. Isn't that right, Jacob?" She balled up the cookie wrapper and threw it away.

Jacob's father had loved baseball, Harry thought as he picked a cookie from the middle of a row. He had died two years ago of a heart attack. So young. Terrible loss. Penny's heart broke that day, and so did his.

"Yep. The coach is going to show me how to throw a better slider. He said my fastballs were great, but my other pitches needed work. What's WAH? You didn't tell me." He glanced at both of them, then repeated, "WAH, WAH, WAH," like someone imitating a baby crying. He then repeated it more slowly like it really meant something.

"Your gram doesn't want you to get hurt if the baseball thing doesn't work out," Harry lied. "It means, 'worried about him.'" That part was true. It was always followed up with one of them checking out the person who worried them; he'd have to do so in this case, too, with the coach. Penny didn't use their code without discretion.

"I'm proud of you and your pitching, Jacob, honey. But you never know." Penny opened the refrigerator. Peering in at the empty shelves, she said, "I do have milk."

"Oh, he wight mum mere."

"Don't talk with your mouth full." Penny grabbed a glass from one of the cabinets, but Jacob ignored it and drank straight from the carton.

Harry watched Penny as she eased back into her seat.

"The coach might come here. He wants to meet the families of his best players. I told him Mom worked all day as a Special Ed teacher and at the restaurant a couple of nights a week, and that I practically lived here. He said he might even come over tonight."

"Yeah? I didn't think anyone did house calls anymore. That's very nice of him." Harry nodded. "So, you're that good?" He took the glass and poured milk into it.

"Yeah, he's gonna help me with my ..."

"He may come tonight, you say? It's already seven-fifteen." Penny glanced at her sweatshirt and leotards. "He'll call first, right?"

Harry smiled at Jacob, who shrugged. "That's really terrific, kid! And what's this coach's name, so I know what to call him when I meet him?"

"Tom Rankin. He's only been at the school for a month. I like him. I'm sure he would like to meet you, too, Uncle Harry. He's a great guy. I bet he doesn't know any private investigators!"

Harry shifted in his seat. "So you throw an eighty-mile-an-hour fastball? That's like the majors, right? Those guys throw faster than Superman flies."

Jacob laughed. "Yeah, faster than Superman flies. I'm gonna tell the coach that one. Maybe the Yankees'll draft me right out of high school and I'll make millions! I'll buy Mom a great big house, and you and Gram could come and live with us!"

"Thank you, sweetheart." Penny smiled.

"Nice of you, Jacob." He patted him on the shoulder.

"Mom says you're quitting your job. Mom says you loved being a private investigator. Mom says Gram loved working with you."

"This one didn't miss a trick when we worked a case together." Penny glanced over at Harry. "He'll be sixty-seven next month and he could still nab the worst of them. He's from Jersey City, you know, the old Jersey City, not this new one." Penny winked at Harry.

"We worked well together. Your gram has a good eye for people." Harry reminisced about his PI service—thirty years of his life spent catching one type of criminal or another, and now he worried about them catching him. Weird.

Just recently, Crystal Joy had begged Harry for help, a regular damsel-in-distress, just like in the old black-and-white TV shows. Of course, Harry couldn't resist a pretty face, half-hidden behind blonde curls, especially when it was attached to money, lots of money. Crystal had taken him for a short ride, unlike the longer one the police chief, James Gibson, had gone on. Ultimately, James Gibson had run down Crystal's husband, killing him. What a mess. Crystal and the dirty-handed police chief had landed behind bars, thanks to Harry's discovery that Crystal had planned the whole caper with the chief. They would kill the old fart and run away with his money. A good old story with a good old ending. Made Harry laugh every time he thought of it.

He was too old for this. Time to settle down.

"Well, kid, that's great," Harry said again. He had lost track of the conversation and glanced at Penny to help him find it again.

"Yeah, it's great." Penny added.

No help there.

"I think I'll go take a short walk, stretch my legs after all that driving," Harry said as he headed toward the front door.

"How's about I go with you?" Penny said. "I could change. Who's following you?"

"Not now. I'll be back in an hour or so, Penny. I'm going over to Adele's. I called her and told her I'd stop by after I got here."

"I gotta get home," Jacob said, "and do homework. I'll see you tomorrow." He grabbed another cookie as he got up to go.

"Yeah, kid. See you tomorrow."

"Bye." Jacob ran out the screen door, waving as he jumped the low hedges toward his house down the street.

Penny followed Harry. "Listen, Harry. I know when something's wrong. So tell me, what's up?"

"Sometimes I think I'm paranoid. I think someone might be following me, or, I don't know, maybe it's payback time. I thought maybe one of the Shermans."

"Sherman? Like Steve Sherman? The one your testimony put away for twenty years?"

"He's dead, Penny. Died in jail two weeks ago. Choked on a chili pepper. It's his wife and son I'm worried about. His wife came into town and walked by the front of the office several times this week. My used-car buddy said she asked about me. They won't find me here. No one knows you live here. We're safe here. I made sure of that. Even checked the car for bugs."

If only he could convince himself they were still safe.

"One good thing," Penny said.

"Yeah, smart planning, like paying cash for everything."

"Where is Sherman's son?" Penny asked.

"Dunno. Couldn't find him."

"Know if he's good at baseball or has a teacher's certificate?" Penny asked.

"No, I don't know that." Harry leaned over and kissed her cheek. "I'll check it out tomorrow. We're safe here. Missed you. If the coach comes, don't let him in. Get his license plate number and remember his description, height—"

"I know, I know, Harry. Just go," she said as she rolled her eyes. "Are you really going to retire?"

"Yeah. It's time. I interviewed a few guys I liked who want my office space and my last few clients. Sent them on a wild goose chase to find me. Winner gets the few clients and the office rental—along with the name. I thought it would be a good test. I thought no one could find me. Now, I don't know. At least we're safe here." He heard himself say that phrase again.

He hoped they were safe there, he thought once again.

"I'll be back in a bit. I told Adele I'd check in as soon as I got here."

"Is everything okay between you two?"

"Couldn't be better."

***

He sat behind the bushes across the street to stake out Penny's house. He wanted to make sure no one came while he was out, or followed him. He'd visit Adele later.

He eyed a gray Mustang convertible pulling up to the curb in front of Penny's house. He snatched his memo pad from his shirt pocket and jotted down the license-plate number; Penny was probably doing the same.

The man went to the door. He was nearly the same height as Penny's five-foot-seven. But unlike her, he was built to knock down brick outhouses. Thick arms hung from his shoulders. Harry imagined Mr. Clean in a black skintight turtleneck and jeans with a broader smile—if that was possible. His shaved head sparkled, and he looked nothing like Sherman's son.

Good.

A small animal scurried in the bushes as Penny opened the door.

"No!" Penny yelled for half the neighborhood to hear, and slammed the door in his face.

He walked toward the Mustang, stopped, turned back to glance at the front door, shook his head, and slid into his car seat.

Harry could see the man sitting inside the Mustang, and imagined the baffled expression on the face of Coach Rankin, if he was Coach Rankin. He chuckled. Penny was a pip. She half-closed the blinds and the flashing colors of the flat-screen TV in the living room flickered through the cracks. Now that he had seen the man and his car, he'd seek him out and have a word with this Mr. Rankin, or whoever he was.

***

"Can you tell us what time he left here?" a voice asked

Penny as Harry shuffled to the bathroom. Harry stopped to listen at the top of the stairs and looked at his watch, 9 a.m. on the dot.

"Ah, around eight," Penny said. She sounded nervous. He wasn't used to Penny sounding nervous. Or did she just sound older?

"You might have been the last person to see him," the voice stated.

The voice sounded familiar; where had he heard that voice before?

"Did he say where he was going? Did he mention the names of any other players he intended to visit?"

Penny explained how Tom Rankin believed that Jacob would go far in baseball. She couldn't believe that someone had shot him in the back. Horrible is the only word to describe it, she said.

Silence.

Penny spoke as if reading from a card: "Detective Daniel Springer, Union Police Department."

"Do you know the whereabouts of your brother Harry, Mrs. Goldman?"

"No. What does Harry have to do with Coach Rankin?" Suspicion rose in her voice and Harry could see her shoulders raise, her head jerk back, and her eyes narrow. She might even add a sideward glance and cock her head to the right.

"His business card was found in Rankin's pocket."

How the hell did one of my cards wind up in Rankin's pocket?

"Well, he's not here. I'm looking for him myself. He owes me money. Let me know if you find him. My eggs are cooking. Goodbye." She then added, "Hey, nice car. Sporty. Red. Looks like one of those speedy ones, like on a speedway. Low, too. How do you ever get into that thing? My knees would break. Must have cost an arm and a leg."

"It's my brother's. Could never own this. Not in my wildest imagination."

"Nice brother. Better than mine. He wouldn't loan me a nichol."

Good going, Penny, Harry thought. That's my girl. He'd call the police department to investigate Detective Springer, and his brother—if he had one.

Tom Rankin had lived here only a month and someone wanted him dead? Harry wondered about the scenarios that would accompany such a situation. Was Rankin someone he didn't remember who was out to get him?

Harry heard the door close. That voice, he thought.

***

Harry headed down the steps toward the kitchen.

Penny opened the front door and checked outside.

"I'm sure no one is out there, Penny," Harry said as he ambled toward the kitchen. "Good line with Springer about me owing you money. You're still sharp as a tack."

"Got the detective's plates. You should check them out." Penny handed him a piece of a small brown paper bag with Springer's plates written on it. "The murder was on the radio. Big news here."

"Murder is big news everywhere," Harry said. Penny followed him into the kitchen.

Harry opened the refrigerator, pulled out the only bottle of soda, and closed the door.

Penny reached for a glass in the cabinet and set it on the table. "How's Adele?"

Harry chuckled. "I've finally asked her to marry me. I'm

going to buy her a ring. She wants a ring, after all these years. Go figure."

"So, you're marrying Adele? I'm happy for you. Mazel tov. Rings cost a lot of money, Harry, like a couple of thousand."

"Two grand? That's nothing. I saw some for twenty!"

"What's this world coming to? My engagement ring only cost fifty dollars. Of course, it was second-hand."

"Yeah."

The doorbell rang. They looked at the door and then at the clock on the CD/cassette player, 11:07 a.m. shone in red.

"I'll get it." Penny opened the front door.

Detective Daniel Springer had returned.

Harry stood open-mouthed when he saw him. "Well, well, well." He smiled wide and approached the detective.

Harry and Daniel shook hands like old friends.

"You son of a bitch! You were so hard to find! I did it. It took me three months, but I did it! I found you! Now you owe me your office chair!"

"Penny, Daniel Springer is taking over the business. He's one of the people I interviewed." He winked at Penny and smiled at Daniel. "I thought I knew that voice, when you questioned Penny."

"And I suspected you were here all along. Figured I might catch you off-guard by returning so soon."

Harry smiled. "You sure did. Congratulations! Now come in here and tell me how you did it. What clue led you to me?" He waved him toward the living room and the couch.

Shit. No one was supposed to find him, especially this guy.

"I'll get the key to the office, right?"

"You do, you do." Harry tipped an imaginary hat. "That was the deal and I honor my deals."

Penny turned to Springer. "You just made up that part about the card being in Rankin's pocket, didn't you?"

"Yes, ma'am. I wanted to see how you'd react." Springer laughed. "Rankin ran out on people he owed lots of money to. They killed him, or so the story goes. We'll know soon enough."

"We made this deal three months ago, Penny." He waved Springer to one of the living room chairs. "Sit. Spill the beans. How did you find me?"

"Would you like something to drink?" Penny asked. "Detective? Harry?"

"No thanks," Springer responded.

"So tell us." Harry felt anxious. "Penny, get me a GIN."

He added after a long beat, "Penny, I changed my mind; make it a can of PIELS. I feel like a beer."

"Hell, Harry. I'll get ya both. You'll probably change your mind again." Penny shivered. "It's chilly in here, boys, I'm going to get a sweater."

Harry laughed and thumbed toward Penny. "She's a character, my sister."

"Honestly, I was going to give up on you," Daniel started. "All the usual routes didn't work. No paper trails. No insurance or licenses to this place. No taxes to this place. I even checked with my cousin in the IRS. How did you do that?"

"I'm not the one who paid them, that's how. So, talk."

"Harry, I traced your family. It was tough going back through Penny's dead son. But I found the obit, went to the funeral parlor, got the general location, phone book, well you know. Sat at her daughter's house, and who did I see? Penny's grandson, who looks just like you. I followed him and where did he lead? Here." A Cheshire-cat grin crept across his face. "Now, I've completed the job—the chase you put me through—and I'm sure you did your homework on me when I came for the interview, so I'll take the key and be on my way."

Penny set a glass on the table. Harry sipped.

"The problem is, the name you gave me at the interview was a cop, Daniel Springer, who worked for your old man many, many moons ago as an assistant, and left him, gone missing. Your real name is James Gibson Junior."

Daniel's face turned hard and his hand moved toward his jacket pocket.

"You stole names and hunted me down because you wanted the key to my office. Why? Because you wanted to get the records I had on your father in my safe. Those records hold the evidence against him. You want to destroy them, so the case will be thrown out."

"I want the key to that office!" Daniel completed the move into his pocket and pulled out a gun. When he looked up, he saw that Penny held a pistol, aimed right between his eyes. A second later, Harry also drew a pistol. Now Daniel was staring down two guns.

"Two can still take one," Harry said.

The doorbell rang. The door pushed open. The police rushed in.

***

A handcuffed Daniel gaped at Harry and Penny, models for placid retirement.

"When did you call the police?" he whispered, as the cop tugged on his arm to leave.

"Oh, after Harry told me he wanted a can of PIELS. That's code for call the police, or Please Initiate Emergency

Legal Services," Penny smiled. "And GIN is code for Gun Is Needed. We were going to make it gun is near at hand, but who ever heard of a GINAT?"

The Ferry

I walked into the gift shop on the Cape May-Lewes car ferry to kill some time sailing from Cape May, New Jersey, to Lewes, Delaware. My sister Marianne had just died, leaving instructions for her ashes to be strewn over the Atlantic in view of the redbrick waterfront McMansion where she lived with her husband, Clinton. Marianne always loved the ocean, and though we lived five hours and several lifetimes away from each other, I was, in a small way, honoring her by riding the car ferry on my way to her funeral.

The man behind the cash register in the ferry gift shop had a twinkle in his blue eyes. His short gray hair was trim, just like the rest of him. We were both around the same height, five-eight. I could feel those eyes on me as I twirled the revolving rack of postcards, as much to ground myself as the boat rocked from side to side, as to look at the photos. Unlike five years ago, when grief made everything blurry and vague, this time it was all sharp and distinct; it was strange how unexpectedly hyperaware I was. I could even see the man's nametag. Joe.

A book of ghost stories sitting high on a wooden shelf met my gaze. I grabbed it and flipped idly through the pages, remembering Clinton crying over my cell phone, telling me that Marianne had "passed away." A car had veered off the road and hit her.

My sister and I were all that was left of the Kowalski family. Mom, Dad, and our older brother Shawn died in a car accident five years ago. My sisterly relationship with Marianne was crushed with them, and for three years we avoided each other, unable to be together without their ghosts invading our space. The few times we met, Mom, Dad, and Shawn hung above us like smog.

She had blamed herself for the accident and could not see that her thinking was irrational. I tried to tell her so many times that everything in the universe had so many causes, but she was beyond reason. I could have been the one to hold up their departure. Mom could have stopped for the coffee she always wanted on car rides.

She didn't want to go out to dinner with them that fateful day. They'd argued briefly before she stayed behind with me. I went out to party with my new Wall Street pals. I was moving out of an old apartment that weekend to my new upscale place near work, and was visiting the folks for a while before they took off for a visit with their friends. Marianne had headed out the door as soon as they left to her boyfriend's house. It was all so normal, until I got the phone call from the police less than an hour later.

Ever since, she exclaimed ... if she hadn't argued with them ... if she'd just gone with them ... if she wasn't even there ... if she'd never been born. My moody, quirky, strong-willed sister disappeared that night. A colorless, placid stranger had replaced her, a person who changed everything she owned from bright blue to black and white, except for her little blue rowboat. She had wanted to explore the world and become a travel writer. Instead, she became a travel agent, and met Clinton, a book editor for Doubleday in New York, a man who edited her life.

Two years later, she knocked on my apartment door and just hugged me. She wouldn't let go. She wanted a sister. She wanted a family. She wanted me, like she always had.

I froze at first. I'd never really reached out to her, but I'd never shunned her either; I mostly felt ambivalent.

She stayed over and we talked, caught up with our lives. She'd just gotten engaged to Clinton. I didn't get a sense she was passionate about him, but what did I know? She wanted a small intimate wedding, but he wanted a quick "I do" at the Justice of the Peace. I asked her what I could give them for a wedding present and she requested a Tiffany crystal pitcher and wine glasses. That request was not from the Marianne I knew. Tia, my secretary, ordered them and had them sent.

So Marianne and I were careful not to ask any deep questions about grief or pain or happiness, but we did reunite, and met a few times a year for dinner.

But I never really opened up to her. I didn't tell her, for example, that the only man I'd ever loved left me after four years, shortly after Marianne and I reconnected, and moved in with another woman two days before my "Dear Jane" letter arrived in my email box. I'd been through too much loss to trust anyone, even—or especially, I suppose—my last remaining relative. What if she changed her mind and left me? I never really opened up to her.

And, as fate would have it, she did leave me.

I worked ten-hour days in a Wall Street brokerage firm right on Wall Street. I rode my bike, played tennis twice a week, golfed on Sundays, and flew my Mooney airplane. I liked all my teammates and partners, although I have never wanted to take up with any of them, let alone settle down with any of them. I guess you could say I was fiercely independent, and okay, or still very, very hurt. Maybe both.

When she married Clinton Templeton III, it was like Marianne had given up. She certainly gave in to Clinton, who didn't like me at all. He had kept her close to his side and didn't seem to appreciate my independence. In fact, he liked nothing about me, especially that a woman made ten times the money he did.

Marianne died too young. Sadness ripped through me when I thought of her gone, and all those moments that could have enriched our lives, now lost, forever.

I placed the ghost stories back on the shelf and meandered over to the toys in a small alcove. The toys were in bins on shelves, like at the penny arcades. On the lower shelf were more interesting plastic collectibles. I picked up a twelve-inch, plastic, triangle tube with dolphins floating in a blue liquid. On the bottom of all three sides were golden lines marking each inch. I slanted it to one side and watched the four plastic dolphins seeming to swim down toward that end. I tilted it back the other way and watched them spin and dip to the opposite end. I smiled. Marianne loved dolphins and anything else that had to do with the ocean. I liked everything that had to do with mountains or the sky.

Joe continued to observe me. Out of the corner of my eye, I saw him edge to the end of the counter, words ready to pounce when I neared.

Two attractive women stepped into the shop. One

coughed to gain Joe's attention. They were both tall and looked liked sisters. The prettier of the two wore dangling Spam earrings, miniature Spam cans on the end of earring hooks. You couldn't miss them and they made me laugh to myself. The women needed directions. Joe sprang into action. I watched as he reached under the counter, withdrew a tattered map, unfolded it, and placed it on the glass counter, smoothing it flat. Then the women hid my view of him, but laughed at something he said.

Over the phone, Clinton sounded like he was on autopilot, like I was just another call he had to make, to invite just anyone to the memorial service. He explained that after the service and the reading of her will, my sister's ashes would be strewn into the sea. The boat would return to a catered meal. Then he said that Marianne had left something for me. It wasn't part of the will, but a birthday gift she had intended to give me. In other words: come to the memorial service, listen to the will, pick up your package, sign on the dotted line, and leave. Fine with me, I thought. I calculated that the whole event would be four hours tops. I looked forward to meeting Marianne's co-workers at the travel agency, and I was certain I wouldn't feel like eating when I returned to shore. I just wanted to see her ashes merge with her beloved ocean.

What could Marianne have for me? When we'd met for dinner two months ago, she said she'd bought me a gift, but then dropped the discussion. We shared so little that meeting. She seemed preoccupied, as though she wanted to tell me something about Clinton, but couldn't bring herself to do it.

What could she leave me? It's not as if she could leave me an old tattered teddy bear that we both snuggled into on rainy nights when thunderstorms raged. I was five years older, and she had been a royal pain-in-the-ass sister to me when she was young: a yelling whiny pain-in-the-ass who demanded my time and stuck to me like a leech. I usually managed to peel her off and hand her over to my mother. Sometimes, when I walked away, she ran screaming into Shawn's arms. My brother had the patience for her during those years.

Joe finished giving directions, even adding an address. The formerly lost souls strode out the door, now assured of a safe arrival to their destination. Joe softly said hello as I stepped up to the cash register and placed the plastic dolphin ruler on the counter. Joe would be the only witness to my buying it. No one would know that I would think of Marianne every time I looked at it sitting on my teak desk, the dolphins staring at the East River.

Joe and I talked. Well, mostly Joe talked. He apologized for taking so long with the tourists, explaining that many of them needed directions. His soft voice never really invaded my space, even though I heard every word, and he then unfolded his life with care to details. He was a seventy-one-year-old retired car salesman and lived in a fifty-foot trailer. He had been alone most of his life. He worked full-time at the gift shop and loved talking with people. Joe spoke like a salesman selling life. He studied my face, and had a knack of looking through me as he spoke, as though he knew all about me without me saying a word. I began to feel anxious, wanting to get back to my seat and look out at the ocean. And he hadn't yet rung up the dolphins.

Then he started with the questions. Uh-huh, I worked. On Wall Street. Yes, a hectic but rewarding life. Yep, a tough market, but I do well. Oh yeah, I'm going to a family reunion (of sorts) for a few hours. I would be visiting my sister (sort of) and her family. Joe didn't have to know that Marianne said they had been trying to have children, and that the hit-and-run shattered that dream, and ended thirty years of her life.

The register finally rang and the drawer flew open. I paid in cash and received my change. Joe nodded politely, bagged the swimming-dolphins ruler, smiled, and hoped I had a wonderful time with my family. As he handed me my package, he studied my tired eyes. I nodded goodbye and returned my thoughts to Marianne and the sea.

Dad had taught Marianne to swim at New Jersey's Seaside Park. We had lots of fun there in those days, all of us. I bet that's why she loved the water so. Marianne had grown out of her whiny phase, and when Shawn wanted to play arcade games on the boardwalk, Marianne preferred to sit on the beach with me and watch the white waves curl in the dark water. I remembered Dad telling me to watch her while he and the others went off for cotton candy and a spin on the wheels of chance. I didn't mind. Marianne had looked up at me with her China-doll blue eyes. Her short wavy blonde hair fluttered in the breeze. She smiled her dimpled smile and held my arm. I kissed her forehead. She was a sweetheart at the ocean. Watching the sea calmed her. It was as if she projected her feelings into the ocean and watched them swim away.

She shared her five-year-younger sister secrets about kids in her class and the boy who was breaking her heart. She had kept loving boys who broke her heart, and grew to like the oddballs of society, or so I called them. I always hugged her when experiences turned her cheerful nature sour, and then let her know her secrets were safe with me, and it would all turn out okay.

Those were the times I had loved her most.

When she got older, she wanted to fly with me. I said no. No one flew with me. I flew alone. I needed to be free.

I suggested that she find something to do that was hers alone and that nobody could take away from her. She snubbed me for a couple of months, but eventually she bought a little blue wooden dinghy, the color of her eyes. She wouldn't let anyone else in it, especially me. I teased her and tried to approach the little boat from all different directions. She kept standing in front of each point of entry. I laughed harder and harder as she blocked me. Finally, I grabbed her and we hugged. I didn't let her go until she laughed, too. I took a picture of her next to that dingy and carried it with me. It was my favorite.

***

Like a welcoming friend, the water gently nudged the ferry into port. As workmen threw ropes around wooden posts, the boat seemed to exhale. I headed down the metal steps to my car. I circled to see if any dents had appeared, but the Porsche remained perfect. I looked in the mirror to refresh my makeup. My hazel eyes shone against my tanning-salon dark skin. I should have washed my short wavy chestnut hair last night, but my dimples still creased with that bright daddy-always-loved-your-pearly-whites smile. Marianne and I had a strong resemblance each other. I studied the chip Marianne had given my front tooth.

It had been at a family baseball game and I was the catcher. We all coaxed Marianne to the bat and Dad taught her how to swing. She swung for the home run, but missed; my tooth caught the tip of her bat and I laughed before I cried. I could have gotten the chip fixed, but I liked the slight character flaw it gave my face. Later, it aided the rough-and-tumble image I needed on the Street. It didn't detract from my looks; my boyfriends loved it.

Within a half-hour, my Porsche slowly descended the ramp into the bright light of noon.

***

As Clinton, taller and thinner than I remembered him, opened the door, the mask of indifference he wore in my presence was chiseled away by sorrow. As soon as our eyes met, however, he pinned back his shoulders, raised his chin, and cleared his throat. He narrowed his small black eyes, and the old veneer hardened on his personality. He waved me in, grunted a hello, and pointed to the den where his lawyer brother, William, waited.

The maid, Jesse, who I barely knew, offered me some manners, a smile, and a stiff drink. I accepted all three. She extended her sympathies, especially for the way my sister had died.

The den was walled in mahogany bookcases filled with books edited by Clinton. His Armani-suited brother, who resembled him in size and stature only, sat behind the mahogany desk holding a Mont Blanc pen. William bent to the floor and produced a blue Nine West shoebox. I wanted to laugh. Marianne was planning to send me a Shoe Box greeting card. It was to be for my thirty-fifth birthday. I gave her a mental thumbs-up. My blue-jean-clad sister was roaring with laughter in an unladylike fashion somewhere in the clouds. I wished we could have shared that laughter together. William muttered his condolences, and patted me on the back.

I accepted the box straight-faced, hiding a secret grin for Marianne's joke. Did Clinton get it? I doubted it. I said thank you, but the memory of the sarcastic humor Marianne and I had both shared suddenly made my heart hurt. I wanted to kiss her forehead and give her a farewell hug.

I picked at the masking tape that Marianne had used to circle the box. Maybe I saw symbolism in everything that day, but I fought another urge to grin. It was just like Marianne to wrap a gift in a used shoebox with the cheapest tape. I brought the box out to my car and scanned the water where her ashes would rest. I spotted her little blue dinghy tied to the dock next to a huge cabin cruiser. I wondered who would use it now.

***

I sat in the Porsche, watching the exodus from the parked vehicles up the metal stairs to the main deck of the Cape May-Lewes ferry. I checked my makeup in the car mirror, then stared at the Nine West shoebox sitting next to the bag with the plastic dolphins. After several minutes, I aimed for the bar and some straight gin with a splash of tonic. It was going to be a long night and I had changed my plans. I'd stay at one of the Cape May inns near the ferry building. A couple more drinks before sleep sounded good to me.

I didn't think it would be this hard. Sure, I had some great memories, but our last few get-togethers, we hadn't had much to say to each other. We stumbled for words, and wound up talking about work and men, and sometimes her classes at the yoga center, but never heart-to-heart. That last time, Mom, Dad, and Shawn were back.

***

At the small bar, I ordered a drink and half-listened to the conversations around me. Then I noticed Joe walk in. He smiled and approached me, while I waited on my next round. He asked me about the reunion and I shrugged. Things never turn out the way you think, and people are never what you expect, I thought. Feeling as though I should say something, I explained that it hadn't gone as well as I had anticipated. He nodded empathetically. He asked me to come to the shop when I finished my drink and assured me he wouldn't keep me for long, he had something to show me.

I thought it odd, and had no intention to return to the shop, but I said I would. The bar filled up and got noisy. I could see the ocean in the mirror behind the football-player-shaped bartender and caught glimpses of myself. I looked awful. I ordered another drink and feeling hemmed in and claustrophobic, got up and wandered toward the gift shop. I hoped Joe didn't allow the drink in the gift shop, so I could leave.

Joe must have had a sixth sense because he spotted me instantly. I nodded to him as I walked in. A little kid pulled at a rubber fish and watched as its tail stretched and then snapped back into shape. The kid laughed and called for his sister. A man tried on caps with the Cape-May-Lewes Ferry emblem, and a little girl ran over to the kid, both giggling as they tormented the rubber fish. Two people stood at the register and Joe placed his forefinger up in the air. I stood next to the postcards and glanced at the ghost-story book I had paged through earlier. Déjà vu. I sipped my drink.

Joe rang up his last customer and waved me toward the back of the store, carrying a plastic bag. I followed. He ignored the drink and skirted around a section of plastic toys that looked as though they might break before they left the shop. Near the back corner was a pencil holder with the same indefinable blue liquid and dolphins as my ruler, with a spot on the front for a slip-in picture.

He placed it in the bag and handed it to me. It was a present, he said. It would go with the other dolphins and I could add my favorite person's picture.

Why would he think the ruler was for me, I asked? I might be buying it for a young niece or nephew.

He shrugged. He wanted to give me something to cheer me up, and the other dolphins had made me smile.

Porsche owners didn't usually buy cheap plastic trinkets. We didn't buy anything not from a designer shop or a pick-of-the-month-rich-man's-special. My wine cost over a hundred dollars a bottle, and my diamond earrings probably cost more than the total of all the products in the store.

I was touched.

He patted my shoulder and gave it a slight squeeze, and wished me a safe trip home. I smiled and thanked him.

I had a passing urge to tell him the truth, to spill the overflowing pain and gush about how I detested Clinton, how I had really loved my younger sister, and how angry I was that our parents had died so suddenly and ended all the relationships in our home. But I merely lifted my drink to Joe in a toast and walked out, sipping.

***

Another three quick drinks later at the bar found me knocking at the door of a Cape May inn. From the row of colorful Victorians, I had chosen the lavender one, my favorite color. When the elderly proprietor saw me wobble into her lavender high-ceiling parlor, I didn't have to convince her that I wasn't fit to drive.

The antique sleigh-bed frame creaked slightly as I

eased onto the mattress in the small flowered-wallpapered room.

I leaned back against the headboard and placed a thick feather pillow on either side of me. Then I rested the shoebox on my lap and began to peel off the masking tape. The lid of the shoebox slipped off easily. The box was filled with family pictures she had promised to share, and a lightweight box wrapped in sky-blue handmade paper. I tried to imagine what could be inside. Under the wrapping was a navy-blue box with Swarovski printed in white letters. I opened the box slowly. Diamond-colors reflected on the walls even in the dim light of the room. Etched in the glass on the tail of the crystal airplane was my call sign, N50992. Tears trickled from my eyes as I read the hand-written gift card attached: To Freedom.

I held the plane for a long time soaring into its endless colors.

Finally, the crystal plane rested on the nightstand next to dolphins swimming around a picture of the young dimpled Marianne the day she showed me her new blue dinghy and wouldn't let me sit in it. I turned off the antique lamp behind the plane and picture, and thanked Joe.

***

I woke up the next morning with a wicked hangover. Merely sliding my big toe out from under the sheet made me groan loudly. My head split in two. I wet my cracked lips with my tongue and tasted the salt of old tears. I didn't have to look in the mirror to know my swollen face held bloodshot eyes, and my hair lumped to one side of my head. Since I always slept on the left side of my face, stomach to mattress, everything on that side flattened.

I edged off the bed, held onto the bureau, and really looked at myself in the mirror. I was right. Everything was as I expected except for the aquamarine-green that flooded my eyes when they were surrounded with red blotches from either crying or drinking. I was nude, too.

There was a knock on the door. Did the innkeeper wait and listen, like a loyal dog, to hear when I awoke? I searched the messy room and spotted the crystal plane and blue-dolphin ruler. My heart ached.

"One moment, please," I yelled.

I searched the closet and found the soft thick Terry robe I hoped would be there. I slid it on and wrapped the belt around my waist and made a bow. I looked like a Christmas present with all the extra cloth of the belt. I cracked open the door and gazed at the grandmother-type innkeeper who took pity on a drunken woman last night and let me stay.

Her gray hair was pinned back into a bun and her over-sized dress either came right out of a very old thrift shop or she'd owned it for fifty years. It had tiny flowers on it that, as I stared at them, started to make me dizzy. Her eyes were light-gray-blue marbles. Too big for her face, I thought. But what really caught my attention was the man behind her: young, attractive, dressed in chinos. He looked Italian. His dark hair was straight and longish; his teeth pearly white as he smiled at me, and a scar along his cheekbone underplayed the devilish gleam in his oak-colored eyes. He stood a head taller than me and could sense, I believed, my trouble focusing.

"Can I get you a cup of coffee?" the innkeeper asked. I forgot her name, if I ever knew it. I couldn't remember much about last night. I remembered the word freedom. Right now, however, I was captured by a hangover and tied to an imaginary ball and chain. I dragged my body through each moment.

"Yes, thank you."

"Oh, this is Detective Mosconi. He'd like to talk to you."

"About what?" I addressed her.

"It's about your sister, Marianne," he said as he peered through my tired eyes waiting for a reaction.

"Oh, I'll be out in a few minutes. Need to take a shower and get dressed."

"Lemon under the armpits helps with hangovers," he suggested.

"Coffee and time help mine, thank you."

***

The long dining room table looked like it came out of a convent—it was that plain and ugly. The oak armchairs must have come from the same sale at the old thrift shop. The seat cushions had obviously accommodated many bottoms, because they sagged too close to the wood for any comfort. I did feel better, however, after the shower, a couple Excedrin from my purse, and my first cup of coffee. I was now out of the fog and into life.

Ms. Grandma poured me my second. I stared at the china cup and wondered if it would get bigger as it got older. Where were the big mugs? The coffee was bitter, but so was life. I sipped some more. I had on the same clothes from yesterday and planned on a quick exit as soon as I found out what the Italian detective wanted to know about Marianne. I exhaled and realized I was hungry. I couldn't remember the last time I'd eaten anything; I knew I drank my lunch and dinner. Grandma must have read my mind, because she placed eggs and bacon in front of me.

"Would you like some orange juice?"

"Yes, thank you." I so appreciated the breakfast and the silence. I loved silence. I ate the eggs and toast and nudged the bacon to the side of the dish with my fork.

The detective came out of the kitchen carrying his own breakfast. Maybe he had a meal plan here.

"Aren't you curious about what I have to tell you about your sister?" Detective Mosconi asked, blowing the silence apart.

"She dead. What else is there to tell?" I wanted to end any discussion as soon as possible. I didn't feel like talking to anyone.

"She might have been murdered."

I dropped my butter knife. I stared at the bacon, trying to process the word. Then I looked up. "Murdered? Sweet, smiling, loving Marianne? Murdered? Why do you say that?"

"A witness saw the hit-and-run and claimed that the car aimed straight for her. It also had no plates, which is suspect. We're investigating whether her death could have been intentional." He bit into his crunchy toast.

"Who was this witness?"

"The man who owned the gas station, the BP, across from the yoga center. He's lived in Lewes all his life, and was closing up for the night."

"Do you believe that someone aimed for her?" I asked.

"From the angle of his view, it is very hard to tell. But we have to investigate. I'd like to ask you some questions before you go back to New York and your swanky apartment." He chewed and talked, but I couldn't see the food in his mouth.

I raised my brow to question him in silence. Swanky?

How did he know my apartment was swanky? Maybe he spotted the swanky Porsche outside?

"I ran your plates. All the innkeepers report people who come in very late and very drunk. It's a way of protecting the innkeepers and sometimes the customer." He sipped his coffee. "Then I used Google Earth."

"Hmm," I muttered.

I didn't believe that Marianne was murdered. I couldn't. That's like killed, I told myself. That's like someone wanting her dead. My brain floated in a sea of brown mud, trying to find its way home. Home was a rational port where thoughts made sense. Murdered?

I picked up my butter knife and proceeded to slap loads of fat onto my fresh-baked roll. I would definitely come back and stay with Grandma if I was in the area and she was alive.

A memory of Marianne sitting on my bed in the new apartment and thumbing through my photo albums flashed in my mind.

My hunger died. I could feel the tears revisit my eyes. I put down the butter knife and stared at Detective Mosconi. "Why would anyone want to kill my sister?"

"Well, Regina, that's what we're trying to find out. I'm sorry if I upset you."

I heard the ground calling to me, and gravity grabbed hold of me. Mosconi must have seen me turn white and lose my balance. He stood so fast that his chair hit the floor as he sprinted over, just in time to hold me up from fainting. He righted me gently, leaving his hands on my shoulders till he was sure I was stable. Grandma ran into the kitchen and came out with a cold wet towel. She placed it on my forehead. I held on to the cloth, rested my head on the back of the chair, and groaned.

"You all right, honey?" Grandma asked.

"Think so." I felt the blood rush back to my body. In fact, my whole body heated up. "I'm going back upstairs."

***

Five hours later, I woke up and felt that my whole body was together again. Grandma tapped at the door when I stepped out of bed. How did she do that? The floorboard didn't even creak. She offered me more bitter coffee in the little cup. I drank it down, then jumped in the shower for the second time that day and put on the same clothes once again. I ran the water in the bathroom sink and brushed my teeth with my finger. Finger still wet, I grabbed my car keys and pocketbook and packed up my special presents from Marianne and Joe. I hugged the bag tenderly for an instant.

I would go home and hire the best goddamn private investigator Tia, my secretary, could find. It would be someone who knew this area, would find that driver, and prove that the hit-and-run had been an accident.

"Sleep well?" Detective Mosconi put down the paper he was reading as I trotted down each step at double the normal speed.

"I was out like a light. But I'm up now. I'm going to hire a PI. I'll get the best person possible to find that driver. Be assured, Detective, I will find out who aimed a car at her and hit her, and if it was intentional."

"I suggest you let me gather up all the information I can from you, get some background, and put the pieces together."

"No offense, Detective, but I'm going to hire someone to help you out. I'm sure you have lots of cases and my guy will spend all of his time on this one. He'll ask every person in Marianne's small town what they were doing that night and what they saw. Someone at that yoga club must have seen or heard something!"

I grabbed a chocolate chip cookie off a dish and bit into it, expecting a crunch. It was soft, gooey, hot, and delicious. The smell alone made me salivate. My eyes must have widened with delight, because the detective grinned.

"They are good. I had three."

"Three? Great. I can have two more."

"Betcha you could have five more." He raised his eyebrows a few times.

"Hmmm ..." I smiled. "Five?" I raised my brows a few times, too.

Grandma heard our conversation. "Would you like another? I can wrap a few to bring with you."

"You're terrific!" I meant every word. "That would be wonderful. I have a long ride home."

"Sure. I'll make you a sandwich, too. What would you like? Ham and cheese? Roast beef?"

"I don't eat red meat. Have any turkey?"

"Yes, dear. Turkey and cheese?"

"Thank you so much. I wish I could bring you home with me." I smiled at her.

She patted me on the back. "You've had a hard time of it, dear."

Yes, I had.

"While you're waiting for your box lunch, would you like to tell me about your brother-in-law?"

Mosconi turned in his seat and placed his hands on his lap as if he would push off them to stand.

"From what Marianne shared, they didn't travel together, but they sailed on his cruiser, hiked, and watched TV shows, or went to movies. Sometimes they would go over to his brother William's house for family parties. Clinton and William are trust-fund babies, very rich, and spoiled from the day they were born. That's how he afforded that cruiser. Clinton's arrogant, and demanding, and moody. Marianne said William is wealthier than Clinton, and she liked those parties. She liked meeting the bigwigs and oddballs."

I reflected back on her call to me right after they married. She invited me to one of those parties, but work smothered me. Was she angry I didn't come? I would've been. Guilt visited me again, and touched my heart.

"No relationship is black and white. There's good and bad in all of us. If it wasn't a good relationship, she must have had some responsibility."

"She hated snobbery," I continued. "She loved blue jeans, little blue boats, the ocean, travel, and dolphins and baseball, especially when she could play. She wanted nothing more than to be with different and creative people. He was never anything she was supposed to marry! Now, leave me alone."

He just sat there, looking at me.

"I'm sorry," I said. "It's just that I feel guilty."

"About what?"

"Not calling her more after our parents died. Not pushing her into therapy to talk about it. Not talking to her about it myself. Not probing more into her life when we met for dinner, and sometimes dreading it. Jesus, why am I telling you this?" Then I felt anxious. My skin felt like it was crawling with ants. "As soon as my sandwich comes out of that kitchen, and as soon as I hug ... um ... Grandma, I'm outta here."

"Grandma's name is Helen. She's lived here all her life

and has always been a kind and giving person. I know. She's my aunt."

"Oh," I felt a bit ashamed here and he must have sensed it. "I really like your aunt."

"Me, too." He stood and went into the kitchen. I heard the muttering and Helen laughed as she wrapped something in noisy paper.

Helen handed me two brown-paper bags. One had the sandwich and the other the cookies. Mosconi glided out behind her and held out a Diet Pepsi.

"We could talk more now, or later. It's up to you, but we're not done."

"Later, after I hire my PI." I vise-gripped the can and pulled it toward me. He smiled that big-tooth grin and I headed out the door.

"Regina, you will have to come back and deal with this," he said in a voice akin to a parent's.

Yeah, that was my intention.

I waved with my back turned. "Thanks, Helen. You're the real life saver." Then I turned around, scooted over to her, and gave her a quick hands-full squeeze around the shoulders and a kiss on the cheek.

"Good-bye, Regina. Have a safe journey. Don't let Steven scare you, and be well. I'm so sorry about your ..."

I was out the door, holding back yet another set of tears.

***

Driving down the West Side Highway, I finished my last cookie. The first set of cookies went within ten miles of the old purple Victorian and Helen. I'd engulfed the sandwich in New Jersey. The Diet Pepsi was another story. Picturing Steven holding it out to me with that cocky grin made me want to throw it out the window. But we Wall-Streeters know when to hold them and when to throw them. I drank it on the New Jersey Turnpike near the Parkway merge. Tiredness had totally overtaken me. I was a zombie. I was fantasizing about a PI (that I hired) killing Clinton. I loved that one. In another, Marianne was still alive and well, and I was hugging her while Clinton watched green with envy. The son-of-a-bitch had gotten the best years of her life.

I passed the 96th Street boat basin and realized I was almost home. If it had been rush hour, it would have taken another hour or two. The sky infused ink-colored clouds into yellow. I would be home within a half-hour.

***

My Ragdoll cat, Kiki, stared at me when I entered my 25th-floor apartment in the Battery. I picked her up—and should have known better than to pick up a cat that is trying to ignore you. She scratched to get down and to tell me that she was angry that I left her: All sixteen pounds of her scurried into my bedroom. I walked down the short corridor, past the front closet on the left, and the beginning of the mauve, black, and white granite kitchen counter on the right to the expansive view of the Statue of Liberty and the East River. I exhaled. I turned left down the hall to the massive 20-by-20-foot bedroom with the bathroom on the right. Marching into the bathroom with the beige-marble-Jacuzzi tub and separate marble shower seven feet opposite it, I turned on both faucets and lit the lavender candles that faced the five-by-five-foot window that framed the yellow glowing East River. I stripped off my clothes and edged into the hot water before the tub was a quarter-full.

The candles cast an eerie shadow on the back marble wall and I leaned my head on the plastic pillow suction-cupped to the back of the tub waiting for the waters to swirl. The jets were the extra strong ones that I paid the extra strong bucks for.

I looked out at the rising half-moon, then closed my eyes. I had a checklist growing in my brain. My compulsive compunction to calculate every detail was now in full swing. I would hire the people who would find my sister's hit-and-run driver. The jets kicked in and the water swirled. I felt the warmth overtake my body and sooth my restless soul.

Clean and clear-minded, I wrapped myself under the covers of my multi-colored bedspread. Diamond shapes surrounded me in teal, white, wine, and navy blue. I eased my head onto my duck-feathered down pillow, then shot right back up. Paper and pen at my fingertips, I reached over to my teak nightstand and grabbed both of them. I jotted a list of what I would accomplish the next day, and finding the driver responsible for Marianne's death ranked second. Finding the right PI held the number-one space. I was not about to think that I could solve this case. But I had enough money to ensure that someone I hired would. I eased my head on the pillow the second time and fell asleep to the purring of my forgiving cat, snuggled next to me under the covers.

***

I took the next day off. Actually, I could take a year off, sit at my computer in the morning, and make ten thousand dollars in four hours. Day traders can make millions. I wasn't that good, but I was sure I'd always live very well.

The brokerage house I worked for paid me handsomely. I did well by them, too.

I called in at 7:30 a.m. to Tia, my secretary, and the only family I felt I had. She had just come back from two weeks with her family in Westfield, NJ. Words sped out of my mouth faster than a racecar. I told her that I would be taking the next week off to help catch that driver. She gasped. She'd known and like Marianne.

I explained the whole sad story and Detective Mosconi's witness.

Tia and I had been together for years, and we were only a few steps from being married ... I mean, we knew each other that well. She knew all the important birthday dates and what to send to those important people. She knew the names of my friend's kids and their birthdays. She scheduled my social life and my business life. I knew why guys ran off with their secretaries. I was a very lucky woman.

"Tia, take care of everything for a week. Clear my calendar, and find me the best PI in New York, New Jersey, and Maryland," I told her as I checked my list.

"Reggie, I'm not sure I can do that today. I have all the other work you gave me."

"Look up PIs first, okay? Do the research for me. Call them and interview them. Call people they worked for. Call our legal department and see whom they use. Then pick two of the best and I'll take it from there. Hell, I might hire both."

"I'll do my best. I'm so sorry about Marianne. I really liked her. Is there anything I can do for you? You want to come over for dinner tonight?" Tia asked. "I know you're talking work, and you're talking fast. I know what it means when you talk fast. I'll start on the PI immediately and get you a list if not tomorrow, with all the research, then the next morning."

"How are you feeling with the pregnancy? Everything okay?"

"Yep, this pregnancy is easier than going to a dentist."

"Great. I'm so excited for you!" Tears formed in my eyes thinking about Marianne and nieces and nephews.

"Thanks, Reggie, that means so much. And you're the godmother! I'll start the PI search this afternoon. Poor Marianne."

"Thanks, Tia. Anything else I should know?" I flipped that last comment off my emotions, along with being a godmother.

"Everyone sends their condolences."

News of my sister's death must have flashed through the brokerage house quicker than a Florida brush fire. I wanted to run away. I was allowed a week's bereavement leave, and I was going to take it, starting now. I dialed Tia back. She answered before I heard a ring.

"Reggie?"

"I'm starting my bereavement leave now. I can't handle everyone looking at me with sad puppy-dog eyes. I thought I could, but I can't. I'm going back to Cape May and check it out myself. I really need to get the whole picture."

"Oh, Reggie! Do you want me to come with you? Don't go alone."

"Nope. I want you to do all my paperwork for the week, call and cancel my appointments, and explain how ..." I had to hold back more tears, "...broken-hearted I am." I knew Tia heard the tone of my voice change. "But I really want you to lay it on thick with the others. Just couldn't handle coming in, blah, blah, blah. I'm not ready to handle the office, and the people, blah, blah, blah." Tears slid down my cheek. "Tell them I loved my sister very much, and she was all the family I had left," I added starting to sound like a croaking frog. I swallowed hard. "And take care of Kiki for a while. Gotta go."

"I'll call you later," Tia said. "Hang in there."

"Yeah." I hung up, then swallowed hard, cleared my throat, then phoned Helen in Cape May and reserved the same room with the antique wallpaper and soft Terry robe.

***

The lavender Victorian sat in a welcoming pose as I parked in front of the house. I felt the smile grow on my face as I envisioned a tuna sandwich followed by fresh homemade chocolate chip cookies. I opened the heavy wooden door and the scent of the baked goods poured into my nostrils. Yes! I wanted to quell my hunger with food and hugs, the latter being just as important as the former.

Helen walked out of the back as I waited in the front, feeling nostalgic about our first meeting. I hadn't even noticed the antiques in the room, and the lovely flowers throughout the house.

"Hello, Regina," Helen greeted me with a smile. "It's so good to see you again." She came around the counter and wrapped her arms around my shoulder. "You look more refreshed this visit." She stepped back and studied my eyes, probing for a reaction. "I have your room ready. Are you hungry?"

"Famished," I responded. "It's great to see you again, Helen, and thank you for being so kind to me on my last visit."

She waved me toward her. "Come. Leave your suitcase here. Joe will bring it to your room. "

"Joe?" I could only think of Joe from the ferry. "Joe from the gift shop on the ferry? You know him?"

Helen chuckled softly. "Yes, the same Joe. Everyone knows everyone here, dear. He visits every now and then. He lives in a trailer outside of North Cape May."

"Oh," I said. The shock must have registered on my face.

"Yes, come, eat. Would you like a turkey and cheese sandwich?"

"Do you have tuna? I've been dreaming of tuna and chocolate chip cookies."

"I do have tuna, and fresh chocolate chips cookies." Helen's chuckle infected me and I giggled.

"You have already made my day," I said, wheeling my luggage out the way of the counter and toward the steps, placing my purse strap over my shoulder. We ambled toward the kitchen. "Steven's not here, is he? I should probably call him Detective Mosconi. Yeah, I feel better with that."

"Call him whatever you like, honey. And no, he'll be here later, for dinner."

I sat on one of the hard chairs with the thin cushions. Helen stood in the doorway to the kitchen. "I may be staying for a week. Is that okay?"

"Yes, your room is available. The season doesn't get going in earnest till Memorial Day. April has been a warm month for us, though. The flowers are coming up already. Everyone will be in for the summer concert in Lewes. There's only three thousand people there, so we get lots of overflow, plus people love taking the ferry the seventeen miles back and forth. Beautiful ride."

I looked around for Joe, but didn't see or hear another person in the house. "How many rooms do you have?"

"Seven. I live up on the third floor."

No wonder she looked so fit.

Helen disappeared into the kitchen. I called after her.

"Can you give me directions to the Yoga Studio? It's on Harbor Way."

"Sure I can. But don't you want to speak to Steven first? Just to see what he's been doing on the case, so your, uh, efforts don't overlap?"

"No, Helen. I'd like to visit the Yoga Studio myself. Maybe I can talk to some of the women Marianne took classes with. Chatting woman to woman might get info that could help."

Helen set the sandwich down in front to me. She set down a second plate next to me. "Joe doesn't know it yet, but a tuna sandwich is his lunch today. What would you like to drink?"

"Water would be fine," I said as I bit into the sandwich. I chewed and swallowed. "Yummy! This is perfect!"

As Helen placed a glass of water in front of me, Joe walked into the room.

"Hello, young lady. It's so good to see you again," he said as he sat next to me. "I placed your luggage in your room. How are you?"

"Better than the last time you saw me. And thank you for your gift. It was perfect. I was touched."

He patted my shoulder. "You're welcome. I know this is a hard time for you. How's the sandwich?"

"Perfect." I had to stop using that word. Nothing in life was perfect, and I most certainly understood that. Get more information about Marianne, I told myself.

"So, had either of you ever met Marianne?"

Silence.

The word perfect melted before my eyes.

"She's been on the ferry," Joe said. "She visited the gift shop several times and I spoke to her. I speak to everyone, or try to, that comes into the shop. I thought you were her sister, but I wasn't certain. When you bought the dolphin ruler, I knew. Marianne had bought the very same one! She told me how much she loved it."

My heart stopped for an instant. Joe knew Marianne. He didn't have any special sixth sense, which I'd credited him with. I couldn't trust my perceptions lately.

"And she did stay next door at Kelli's once or twice," Helen added.

"Do you know why she stayed at Kelli's when she lives, or lived, in Lewes?"

"Spat with her husband, as far as Kelli could tell. She said she was taking a few days outside of Cape May. She came back a few days later, but stayed at Kelli's for the night ..." She trailed off, though it seemed to me she wasn't finished.

"Go ahead, tell her," Joe said.

"She, uh, had a man with her the second time at Kelli's."

Marianne having an affair? That was news to me. "Do you know the man's name?"

"No, sorry." Helen seemed to be getting uncomfortable. "I do know that they stayed in separate rooms."

"Enough questions," I said, deciding not to involve them any further. I changed the subject to the history of Cape May, Lewes, and the Victorians.

"Lewes," Helen said, "was the first town of the first state of the union, Delaware, and settled in 1631 by the Dutch. It's still preserved as a historic nautical village and is at the intersection of the Delaware River and the Atlantic Ocean. Did you know that?"

"No," I said. I knew nothing about either Cape May or Lewes.

"I'm going into Lewes, too. Can I ride with you into town? I'll show you some of the historic houses from the 1600s, and direct you where you want to go," Joe asked.

"Sure! That would be great."

***

Can you fall in love with a ferry on the third ride? I did. I rested on the same seat I had the first go around and thought about Marianne, the funeral, Clinton, and the little blue boat, while Joe left to talk to friends.

Was her funeral only four days ago?

I felt as if the ferry cradled me protectively, the rhythm of the sea rocking me gently. People's voices murmured around me, and I closed my eyes.

"Regina. Regina. Wake up. Time to get off." Joe shook my shoulder.

"Huh?" I awoke with a start and gazed around me. The boat was just as I had left it in my waking life, cradled once again into port. I slept so soundly that a huge bulk of time passed in a second, maybe two. I felt renewed, ready to learn more about my sister's life ... and death.

Joe right behind me, I ambled to the Porsche, smelling the sea air and blinking into the sunlight. I cherished a few mindless moments watching sparkles dance on the little waves atop the vast ocean, an unseen seagull squawking to an endless sky. I knew how it felt, I thought, as my mind motored up to face the day.

I dropped Joe off to meet a friend at Bes'eme on Market after a brief tour. The colonial town of Lewes, with its

Victorian houses and quaint business center, charmed me. I would have to explore it further, but for now, I drove toward Rehoboth Beach to the Yoga Studio off the coastal highway. The busy street seemed tranquil enough and the speed limit was 25 mph. I wondered where exactly she was hit. In front of this store? That tree? How many people were around? Did any try to help, or did they just stare? Only one witness? Yes, it was dark, but still. How much did the detective know?

I placed my brain on hold as soon as I smelled the soothing sandalwood incense in the Yoga Center. I stepped up to the counter with two beautiful yoga-clothing models engrossed in the full chart of events, pointing to what appeared to be the next class.

"Oh," the taller one noticed me, "hello, can I help you?"

"Yes, I would like to speak to the manager. Is he or she in?"

The young lady, I guesstimated to be around twenty-five, studied my face. I was sure she was questioning my resemblance to Marianne, the dimples, the short wavy hair, and the face structure.

"Are you related to—"

"Yes, I'm her sister. May I speak to the manager?"

"The owner is here, but not the manager. She's off today. Would you like to speak to the owner?"

"Sure."

She waved me to a cloth seat behind a round coffee table. "Can I get you anything? We have—"

"No, thanks." I held up my hand and smiled.

A class must have just started, because the waiting room was empty. I studied the clothing hanging on racks on the opposite wall, and the soothing colors of the walls;

the New Age music was barely audible. It felt more like a spa than a yoga studio. I leaned my head back, shut my eyes, and thought about Marianne here, standing at the counter, paying for her classes, meeting friends, and laughing at some of the yoga poses. I could almost walk in her body, go through the motions of her life, and feel her presence. Now she was with Mom, Dad, and Shawn.

"Hello, Regina." My eyes shot open, and in front of me stood William, Clinton's brother with the swanky suits and the even swankier pens.

"William?" How could I hide my surprise? "You own this place?"

"Yes, the business and the building."

"Marianne was killed in front of your yoga center?"

"Yes, I'm sorry to say, she was."

"Did you know Marianne well?"

He looked at me and I could see his lawyer's mind working, but before I had a chance to wonder what he was thinking, he said, "Yes. She's, uh, was my sister-in-law. Marianne was close to my wife Peggy. And she came here often, four nights a week. She wanted to be an instructor. But I suppose I didn't know her that well, because I was surprised when Clinton told me he wanted the police to investigate the hit-and-run also."

Could there be no love lost between the brothers? "Why were you surprised?"

"Didn't you know? He was seeking a divorce from Marianne. They were separating."

"No." I felt terrible admitting it. "I didn't know."

I thought they were happily married and working on having a family, and that she rowed her little blue boat to feel free when they weren't out on his cruiser drinking Rum Runners and making mad passionate love in the sun.

For the most part, she made me think her life was wonderful. Didn't she? Or was that what I wanted to hear? Had I missed noticing the mask she held up between us? What cloud did I live on? My now beleaguered mind tried to wrestle with this new information

"Would you like to step outside and talk a bit more?"

Man, did I feel foolish. "Sure, let's take a walk." I could barely lift up my head as I examined the lines in the concrete sidewalk. I didn't notice the scenery, the stores, the sky, or the street. "How long have you owned this business?" I asked. He was wearing elegant shoes and navy-blue slacks, and I had opted for my jogging sneakers, white tennis socks that touched my black stretched jeans.

"About three years," he lowered his voice to a compassionate tone. "I got bored with law, and it came up for sale. Peggy suggested we buy it. Yoga has really taken off in America."

"God, William, I didn't even know about Marianne and Clinton." I thought I would cry on the spot.

"Well, I'm sure you knew it wasn't exactly a match made in heaven. Clinton's so ... introverted, cooped up in the house editing all day. And Marianne's, uh, was so outgoing. I was surprised it wasn't Marianne asking for a divorce."

"William, was Marianne having an affair?"

"Funny, the cops asked me the same question, and I have to say, not that I know of. She and Peggy were close and Peggy denies it. Plus, Marianne worked at the travel agency over forty hours a week and took four classes a week at night, and started co-teaching. I don't think she had time for an affair."

I started to cry. Thinking of Marianne on that little blue boat, now alone, and maybe not feeling free, but captured. It killed me. I pointed to my car across the street. We never even talked about her riding in her boat. God, I never broached the subject of her riding in her little blue boat! It was the object that united us even though I never rode in it; the object that allowed us to share one of our greatest moments of closeness.

"I gotta go," I said. "I'll stop by again."

"Anytime, and you take care."

I headed for my car, unlocked the door, settled into my seat, placed my head on the steering wheel, and tried to pull myself together.

I rolled down the windows and smelled the fresh clean sea air of spring. I concentrated on my breathing.

I drove back toward Front Street via Savannah Drive. I passed a hospital sign and wondered if that was where my sister had been declared dead. As if Marianne had grabbed the wheel, the car turned toward their house and the water. I needed to talk to Clinton.

Clinton's jaw dropped when he opened the door. The face once chiseled by sorrow was now aglow with relief, or so it appeared. Was he relieved she was dead?

"Hello, Reggie. This is a surprise. Would you like to come in?" He stepped aside and held the door. I had no choice but to step inside. I followed him through the living room into the solarium and looked out over the shore and sea.

Once settled, Clinton looked at me expectantly. I came right out with it. "Why were you and Marianne separated? Is it true you wanted a divorce? Didn't you love Marianne anymore? I thought you wanted to have children. I really thought you loved her."

Both our eyes roamed around each other's faces as if the truth could be found somewhere between freckles.

Clinton took a deep breath, let it out slowly, then said, "Actually, Reggie, Marianne left me a long time ago. The divorce was just a legal formality—"

"But—"

Clinton looked over at me, waiting for my objection. But what objection could I raise? Any argument was simply inserting myself into a world I knew nothing about. Was I there just to absolve myself? Or to hear the truth? Or both?

"I'm sorry. Please. Continue."

"At first, she stayed longer at the agency. Then she got involved at the yoga center, three, four, sometimes five nights a week. Then she started staying away for days at a time. I know she resented that I was always 'chained to the keyboard,' as she called it, and that I didn't want to travel with her, but I thought she loved the house, the boats, the water, and me. Apparently not. So I sought my own counsel and initiated divorce proceedings."

"When was this?"

"About a month ago."

"And you had no idea what Marianne was doing or where she was going when she wasn't home? Did you ask or confront her?"

"Of course I did! But she wouldn't tell me. She said she couldn't. I asked other people, too. This is a small town and everyone knows everything."

"Except if one of the town's people ran over her with their car."

"Does that really matter now?" Clinton asked and shrugged.

I wanted to ask him if he thought she was having an affair, and I almost blurted it out, but I caught myself in time. Instead, I said, "Well, I'm going to talk to Detective Mosconi now."

After Clinton closed the front door behind me, my brain locked and I just wanted to get back to the inn. I was amazed at how differently I felt about Clinton after hearing his side of the story. Marianne had delivered an invisible "Dear John" letter, very much like my "Dear Jane" letter, and he shut down. His sailboat was his plane, and his work grew to be his life. Marianne had apparently been writing their story, and began editing Clinton out of it.

Nothing Clinton told me suggested murder. He obviously had grounds for a divorce, emotional abandonment or whatever it was called. Maybe he even knew she was having an affair. God, did my little sister really have an affair? Tiredness sucked the energy from me. I wanted to talk to Joe again. He saw Marianne and her friend on the ferry. What information did he give Detective Mosconi? I was filling in gaps about people I didn't know and had been wrong.

I returned to the lavender house. I could talk to Mosconi later. And most importantly, tomorrow, I had to go to the travel agency. I had been postponing it, and wouldn't allow myself to think about it. Would they expect me to clear out her desk?

***

I walked into the Inn after the ferry ride back, waved to Helen, who was talking to another patron in the sitting room opposite her counter, and trudged up the long flight of stairs to my room. I dropped my purse on the bed next to the suitcase, pushed everything over to one side, and plopped on top. I stared at the tiny flowers on the wallpaper and breathed deeply the salty air pouring through the double-hung windows. I would rest my eyes and my mind, then take a shower, and then write down every question I could think of to ask Mosconi. I imagined a chocolate chip cookie and coffee, and felt hungry. Yeah, a tough afternoon called for cookies and coffee.

The sound of a bird tapping at the window awoke me. Eyes blurred, I rubbed them and gazed out the window. There were gray clouds, but no bird. How long had I been out? The tapping occurred again, but it was the door. I pulled the tussled sheet over me. "Come in," I called.

Helen had brought a tray with two chocolate chip cookies and hot chocolate. She placed them on the table in front of the window, then headed toward the door. "You've been up here for two hours. You must be hungry!"

"It's been a tough afternoon, Helen. Thank you so much. You always seem to know what I want."

Helen smiled. "Steven just arrived. We are having dinner at six-thirty. Join us."

She must have guessed I was clueless as to any worldly reality at that moment.

"It's five-fifteen now."

"Thanks," I said. An overwhelming feeling of loss rushed over me. Helen's nurturing reopened the wound of Mom's passing, of all of Mom's tenderness, gone.

"I'll let you rest." She closed the door.

I pulled my legs over the side of the bed, stood, and headed for the shower. Just as I turned on the water, my cell phone rang. Tia's ring. "Hello, Tia."

"Hi, Reggie. Are you all right? How's it going down there?"

"It's hard, Tia. Very hard. Opening all kinds of wounds."

"I'm sorry. I really am. Do you want to hear about the PIs?"

Jesus. I'd forgotten all about the PIs. They seemed to reappear out of some previous lifetime. I didn't really want to hear about them, but I also didn't want Tia to think all her work was wasted. "Sure," I said.

"Two stand out from the rest. One works for us, and the other works in Ocean City, Maryland. I thought they were the best of the bunch I interviewed. Have a pen?"

"Yes, but hold on." I moved toward the bed and night-stand and grabbed my notepad and pen. "Shoot."

Tia rattled off the two names and numbers. "If you need anything else, call me. Please. I can be there tomorrow if you want extra support."

"I don't know what I'd do without you," I said. "Thank you, but I think I'll be all right. I just have to reach the end of this trip, and the journey of understanding my relationship with Marianne." I clicked off.

The shower felt good. So did the Terry robe. Hope had returned to my court, and my life felt brighter. I ate the cookies and gulped down the cold, hot chocolate. Six o'clock. Time to get ready.

I skipped down the steps and turned toward the living room, smelling the sizzling fat from the chicken. The dining room table was set for three with what appeared to be Helen's best china. No surprise that there were little light blue flowers surrounding the borders of each plate. Nope.

"Hello, Regina."

I looked around and saw the man of the hour coming in from the back porch. "Hello, Detective Mosconi."

"Steven, call me Steven, everybody does. Come. Join us. Want wine? Beer? Soda? Milk?"

"Wine, white, preferably Chardonnay."

"In the fridge behind you. Glasses, top right cabinet."
He turned back to the porch.

I poured myself a huge glass of wine and moseyed out
the back door onto a fieldstone porch, adorned with lawn
chairs and tables, fresh cut flowers on each of the two-
chair tables that edged the border of the screened-in patio,
and a large table for eight near the modern grill. "Nice grill.
Beautiful patio!"

"Yes. I love it." Helen sipped white wine and grinned.
She was the picture of contentment.

"So, Detective Moscani, can we talk?"

He smiled, waving his hand toward me. "Ladies first."
He placed his hands under his chin and leaned on them.
"We're all ears."

Helen sipped her wine.

"Not much to tell. I spoke to William at the Yoga Center. Then I visited Clinton at the house. They both told
me things I didn't know about my sister, but nothing that
might point to her being murdered." I sipped the wine to
gather my thoughts. "Did you speak to Joe about the man
on the ferry with Marianne?" I asked. "Did he see her with
a man?"

Helen departed to the kitchen and prepared the meal.

Joe's observations of the man numbered first on
Steven's list. "Marianne rode the ferry more frequently
the month before her death, with her male companion at
her side. They sat at the bar. The only bit of conversation
Joe overheard when he passed them included the phrase:
'How are you going to handle the women?'

"Joe described the man," Steven continued. "Average
height, average weight, light brown hair, angular chin,
clean shaven, no scars or broken noses. Dressed in nice,

but not expensive, clothes. Nothing flashy. A goddamn everyman, except for the ice-blue eyes."

We moved to the dining room as Helen served the meal.

"So odd, really," I said. "How many times had Joe seen this man?"

"He thinks around seven or eight times, but in the last month, three, always on a Tuesday. It's human nature to pay more attention after the fact. We all take a lot for granted while we're moving through our day. And he only started wondering the last two times."

As if a silence bell had rung, we all seemed to voyage within ourselves, parting to different planets, light years away from a hit-and-run, a ferry, a man with ice-blue eyes, and the life of a young woman, snuffed out prematurely. The silverware clicking on the china plates was our only music. I knew about taking life and relationships for granted, and paying more attention after the fact. Of course, I was only wondering now. Poor Marianne. Poor Clinton. No person is left unscathed from a bad relationship.

Steven broke the silence. "The man with the ice-blue eyes? He was on the ferry Tuesday. Joe saw him roaming around the ship, like he was looking for someone."

"Well, then, he didn't kill her," I said.

"Not necessarily. There are many reasons he would be there."

"What about the travel agency where she worked? Did you question them?"

"They were first on our list. We wanted to go through her desk, but they said that Clinton had already taken everything. No one knew anything about the hit-and-run, but everyone there liked her. Clinton didn't want them at the funeral, so he was on their shit list. I can't imagine why. He's building a very odd profile for himself."

I understood more about that profile than most.

"So, where does all this leave us?"

"Other than Clinton, that's only because he seems so angry, and some questions about women meeting her at the center, oh, and old Harry at the gas station, it's beginning to look more and more like an accident. We're still putting all the pieces together. It was only six days ago that she died, and four days ago that the witness came forward. Three days ago, we ordered the manifests from the boat and we're tracking down names, and following up leads on businessmen and women, and tourists, who are not many at this time of the year, thank God. Yesterday, we canvassed the area and questioned the neighborhood around the Yoga Center and their home. We're doing all we can because we can't find that damn driver, but I should tell you that the brass is pushing for accidental death. They're giving us till next Wednesday."

"I've been feeling so foggy about all this. Everything I thought I knew about Marianne has turned out, well, to be otherwise. I really didn't know her at all."

"Don't be too hard on yourself. Death makes us all take a good look at ourselves. And everybody has their secrets. Speaking of which," he paused, "have you hired the private investigator?"

"No, I haven't."

"I'd like to make a suggestion. Why don't you ride the ferry on Tuesday? We'll back you up. Maybe the guy with the ice-blue eyes will be on it. If so, we can find out how he fits in, if at all. If nothing shakes loose, we'll close the case Wednesday and then you can hire your PI, if you still want to. How's that sound? It's only two days away."

"Sure," I said. I finished my meal.

"Good. Let's eat dessert." He pulled a business card from a holder in his back pocket. "Call me anytime."

I nodded as I sipped the coffee Helen had poured. It was delicious.

***

I wasted no time the following morning getting ready for a long day of asking several people lots of questions. I prepared for the cool weather that had returned overnight and, according to the forecast, planned to stay. My Coco Chanel bag was now full with scarf, sweater, water, and pull-on galoshes. I consumed breakfast and lunch in one meal, which had Helen laughing. I wished we lived closer. I accepted that she gave me what I missed in not having a hometown mom, and decided to enjoy it. She made me a thermos of hot chocolate that I already knew tasted great cold.

I stood on deck and leaned against the railing to watch the ferry depart the port. I loved the sounds of the ferry next to her home station, rocking gently as if trying to awaken.

Another man was behind the counter in the gift shop, older, and reading a book while he waited for customers. He glanced up at me and didn't move as I entered.

"Will Joe be in today?" I asked, surprised not to see him.

He stared into his book. "Nope, took the day off. Try tomorrow."

Why did Joe take the day off? "Is he okay?"

"Sounded fine to me." The man kept his eyes on his book.

I wandered around the boat the whole trip, studying

people and behaviors, trying to guess what they did for a living or where they were from. It made me think a different way. Stocks and trading were so mathematical. Forecasting trends was fun. Guessing gold futures became an art I could master. But people? People required patience and understanding, and so much more than I had to offer—which I was finding out in spades on this trip. Driving off the ramp and into the sun made me feel that I was now part of the Cape May-Lewes ferry life. I drove straight to the travel agency. Now that Clinton had cleared out her desk, all I had to do was look at it, and meet her colleagues at the office. She had spoken about them and her trips abroad with the old Marianne exhilaration.

The agency was near Lewes Beach, not far from their house off Pilottown Road. I parked next to another Porsche in their parking lot, and took a deep breath before entering. I remembered Marianne describing the people and the place, but I felt ashamed that I remembered so little of it.

Two people sat at the front desks. My office dwarfed theirs. Coffee machine, water cooler, sweets, and packets of different types of sugar and powdered creamers lined a long, narrow counter against the back wall behind Marianne's desk, the empty one in the back. The colorful posters of famous towns and cities from all over the world crowded the walls, adding life and charm to an otherwise dreary room.

"Excuse me," I tried to gain the attention of the man to my left. He looked like Marianne's friend, well, at least how she described him: middle-aged, balding, thin, with a broad smile to fit his broad personality, and dark green eyes.

The man looked up and did a double take. He stared at

me, rose from his seat, came around his desk, and gave me a big hug. "Oh my God, you're Regina. Regina! Marianne's sister! Oh my God, it's so good to meet you! I'm—"

"Jerry. Jerry Walsh. Marianne was so fond of you." That was it. Tears poured out of me and my vision blurred. He started to cry, too.

The lady rose then, and joined us. Jerry stepped back and she hugged me, too. She was the owner, Marge. "I'm so sorry Clinton didn't let us come to the funeral. We would have loved to have met you, and have seen Marianne's ashes swim with her dolphins." Tears dribbled from her eyes also. "That bastard husband of hers! He told us to stay home, and we wouldn't be allowed on his property!"

Maybe he had trouble seeing all the people she loved, and knowing he was no longer one of them, I thought.

"We had our own service at the same time he announced hers would be! Here, come here." Marge grabbed my hand and pulled me to the back of the office and through a stand-in-one-place kitchen. Jerry blew his nose and followed us. On the wall was an "In Memory" collage of Marianne, with her dates of birth and death on the top, and a happy dolphin on the bottom. Pictures of her at work, making faces at the camera, her little blue boat, in France with Jerry, a dog she must have owned, other people in the office, a few Christmas parties, and one very old one of us sitting on my bed, shoulder to shoulder, the day I moved into the New York City apartment, boxes all over the bedroom.

"Lots of our clients and Marianne's friends came. They were pouring out of the front door. People came from the women's shelter too."

"Women's shelter?"

Marge looked at me, as if making sure I was Marianne's

sister. "Yes. Didn't you know about it? The shelter for the abused wives of alcoholics. She donated a lot of money and almost all her free time to it. She even stayed overnight there—"

"Well, we think she did, anyway," Jerry explained, cutting his eyes at Marge. "She sometimes showed up for work in the morning in the same clothes she wore the day before ..."

That was it. My heart sank to my stomach and my knees weakened. Jerry grabbed my arm and brought me to his chair. A half-hour passed before we could compose ourselves. All three of us bonded in the invisible space where Marianne's love still presided. I missed her so much it hurt. I really hadn't tried hard to break her shell of protection, her mask of confidence. I didn't confront her because I knew I couldn't handle her response. Her pain would be too great for me because it was my pain, too, which I also hadn't dealt with. I was selfish. I whispered my apology to her, then cried harder.

***

Steven called Helen's house twice the next day to talk to me. I stayed in my room, spoke to Tia twice, and had her try and find the shelter that Marianne supported. I Googled every keyword I could imagine. No luck.

"Reggie. Those places are supposed to be secret. That's why they're shelters!" Tia reminded me.

Helen brought me breakfast, then lunch, then a snack. I knew she was concerned about me, not coming out all day.

I thought I had finally found the shelter, and called. Nada.

Late in the afternoon, sitting on the bed with my computer resting on my lap, there was a knock at the door.

"Aunt Helen and I are having some wine and cheese," Steven announced. "Would you like to join us?"

"Tempting, thank you, but no."

"Why don't you come down and join us?" Helen said. "You can't be happy cooped up in that room." I opened the door and Helen smiled.

Steven handed me a glass of wine. "Let's go on the porch. It's warmer today. I made crab cakes."

"You cook?"

"Yes, I cook, and pretty well, too."

"Anyone cooks better than me," I said. "Crab cakes? Wonderful."

Daylight dimmed, candles were lit, and more wine was served. The crab cakes tasted divine, and I finally opened up about the sad day and what Marge and Jerry had told me.

"I've been looking all day, but haven't found the place," I said.

"Your sister sounds like a great lady," Steven said.

The candlelight shining on his face softened his looks and sweetened his smile. He placed one hand over the other and held up his chin, elbows resting on the table. Helen excused herself to clear the table and clean up in the kitchen. The conversation eased into talk about his family and friends, my job and colleagues, college for me and the police academy for him, my life in New York City, and his in Delaware. At first, I figured he was being polite, keeping me company in my bereavement. But as the candles burned down to their holders, I began to believe he really did enjoy my company. Saying good-night, I had the urge to hug him, but I fought it and just smiled at him, then headed up the stairs. My feelings were filling up and spilling over. My heart was opening in strange ways.

***

The ferry rocked, the currents curled over in whiteness with the wind, and the sky threatened rain. Great, I thought. Just what we needed as I tried to hold my balance. I knew I didn't get seasick, but wasn't sure I could be around those that did. No one sat outside, which made the search for ice-blue eyes easier. Joe greeted me as I visited the gift shop, surprised to see me.

I moseyed through the ghost books and smiled at Marianne's dolphins. After idling awhile at the cheap toys and walking the short aisles, I left. The bar was the place to hang and meet people. I sat on a stool and ordered, like the first night, a gin and tonic. I glanced at Steven, sitting in one of the booths, playing solitaire with a beer in front of him. He spotted me, eyes wide and cocked his head, touched his ear and spoke.

It didn't take long before ice-blue eyes sat next to me. The ship had evened off and the pitching had decreased.

"God, you look just like your sister." When I smiled, he added, "Well almost."

"It's the front tooth, right? Did she tell you how I got it?"

"Baseball. Your father taught her how to swing a bat, and she hit you in the mouth. Must have hurt."

"It hurt like hell," I answered. She told him that story? They must have gotten very personal. "Tell you other stories about us?" I asked.

"Some. She wanted to call you a thousand times, but always chickened out."

"Why?"

"She was disappointed with her life and didn't want to suck you into it. She hated what she had become and didn't want you to see it and be disappointed in her. She was an alcoholic."

I gasped. "You came here to tell me my sister was an alcoholic?"

"Yes."

He said it so matter-of-factly that it hit me like a hammer. Such a simple word, yes, that summed up everything about Marianne. I finally understood. I didn't need further details, and ice-blue eyes sat with me in silence for so long that I knew he wouldn't offer anything unless I asked. For a long while, I didn't feel like speaking; I just wanted to rest in the embrace of the ferry, cradled by the water, and covered by the sky.

Finally, I said, "So you can tell me where the shelter is." It wasn't a question.

"Yes."

There it was again and though I probably should have been filled with grief, or relief, or guilt, or all of them, I felt curiously uplifted and complete, like one of Helen's flowers, cracking open over sandwiches and cookies and crab cakes, letting in light and life from Steven's attention, and finally blooming in all its glory in locating the missing link to Marianne. "Please," I said, "tell me more."

"I met Marianne at an AA meeting. It'd taken her two years to hit bottom. She blamed her drinking on the accident, but she learned that was bullshit, of course. Only you can drive yourself to drink. Slowly, she overcame the alcohol, then the accident, and finally her marriage. That's when she started volunteering at the shelter for abused women."

He paused and I could tell he was weighing his next words. I waited for them.

"We were working on a new shelter, one for the abused wives of alcoholics—we met lots of them at meetings, because they become alcoholics themselves."

"You said you came today to meet me. How did you know I would be here?"

"Joe."

"Joe?" I should've known.

"Marianne and I attended the Tuesday early-morning meeting in Cape May. She liked to ride the ferry and I, well, I liked to be with Marianne. Of course, Joe knew about it. He knows everything that happens on this boat."

"Everything? Including the shelter?"

"Yes. He's also part of the shelter network. We keep it confidential, although he did tell me about the questions a detective was asking, and what he said."

"Nice of him to help. I'll help from now on, too," I said. "What's your name?"

"Evan."

"And how are you involved in the new shelter?"

"I'm an accountant. I'm doing all the paperwork. I also handle the funding."

"Well, I'll support it, too. Maybe I'll fund the whole project. Just so long as we name the program after Marianne in some way."

Evan smiled. "It already is."

I started to cry. In the end, Marianne was the brave one, not me. She fought her alcoholism, confronted her fears, and started a shelter. She obviously opened her heart to Evan and I didn't really care what else they were to each other. It was none of my business anyway. She even had the strength to leave Clinton.

I'd also never really reached out to anyone, hiding behind my own addiction to work and money. I was the scared one. I felt so ashamed.

***

Steven handed me the Chardonnay and Evan the soda. Helen nibbled on a crab cake next to Joe, who just sat and beamed. Jerry and Marge perched on the uncomfortable chairs around the table, red wine in hand. Steven had closed the case for secondary manslaughter, although the police would keep looking for the hit-and-run driver, probably drunk. I would wait on the PI investigation. Give everything some more time, and it would give me a reason to visit Helen and the crew. Next time, I would fly down.

"I want to make a toast," Evan said, "to Marianne Kowalski and her shelter for victims of domestic crimes, The Little Blue Life Boat."

Everyone clinked glasses and Steven winked at me, then smiled his candlelight-soft smile.

A few tears trickled down my face. It felt like the last of them. How could there be more?

So many new friends, almost a family, and so much love for Marianne surrounded me. I imagined her rowing her little blue boat in the sky, with all the happy dolphins frolicking free.

"To Freedom," I toasted her.

Made in the USA
Lexington, KY
23 March 2014